THE FORBIDDEN FRUITS
RIJU R. SAM

PUBLISHERS NOTE

This novel is a work of fiction. Any references to places, historical events, real people, or real locales are used fictitiously. All names, characters, incidents, places and dialogues are products of author's imagination and are not to be construed as real. Any resemblance to personals living or dead is truly fictional and coincidental.

THE FORBIDDEN FRUITS
All Rights Reserved
ISBN: 978-1-312-32322-3

Written By: Riju Raju Sam
Converted to Book format by: Meetu Nayyar
Designs: Avinash Kashyap
Business Representation: Rosely George, Esq.

Business Enquiries
Dream Merchants, P.O Box 250938, Glendale, CA 91225
Email: dreammerchantsusa@gmail.com
www.rijurajusam.com

Contents

The Seen and The Unseen

The Seen and The Unseen

Isn't it surprising how we refuse to believe what we do not see? Rather as humans we tend to go to any extent to assert that what we see, what we can touch is what exists. We believe that the world of darkness does not exist and forget that light exists only in the absence of light!

We do not believe in spirits and devils or rather we do not want to believe in them. Once again we forget that our belief has no impact on their existence. We are blind to a world that exists right before us. We reject it because we cannot prove it. This is completely understandable. It is natural to think that way............unless God decides to open your eyes to heaven...........and hell, angels.............and demons. The fact that it is not visible to the human eye does not mean it is less real.

The incidents that took place in a remote and a peaceful town of Bridgeport stand testimony to the fact there exist two worlds – one that we can see and the other that we cannot and that the present and future are based on past!

Chapter I

The Seen World

It was a beautiful, sunny Sunday evening in spring. Somehow, the season had an effect on Bridgeport that made even the most haphazardly-sown seeds blossom. The garden in front of the Church stood testimony to the fact. Any time Father Mario was not conducting a service or studying in his office, he was in the garden instructing the gardener or working along with him. The path to the Church was beautiful, as if it was the very road to heaven.

In this small town where everyone knew everyone, the quaint, simple lifestyle pleased the locals who loved their unhurried lives. Today, there was a lot of restlessness in the air. People were huddled in small groups and were busy talking. People walking in and out of the Church looked at the group and even stood to join one or the other group. The topic of discussion amongst the groups was common – happenings in the city in the last few days. While some one talked about people who had gone missing from the town in the last few days the others were discussing the dug up graves and stolen articles from the church. Except for the children who were busy playing everyone was anxious and worried.

Inside the Church, Father Mario, the middle aged priest, was talking to a group of people sitting on a pew. Rachel, the youngest of all was busy enjoying a lollipop, her golden hair tied away from the sticky mess in two pony tails. She was sitting next to to her mother Grace and anxiously fidgeting with a napkin in her hands. Steve who must be few years elder to Rachel sat in the pew with his parents. He was looking at the lollipop in Rachel's hand and just close to them sat Shirley and Joe Mathew. Shirley held on to Joe. Her big eyes open wide would dart towards any movement in the hall. An unknown danger lurked close by, and they were not deceived by the normalcy their eyes could see around them.

"I am sure most of you have noted the odd occurrences in the last few months. There is something unusual happening in the town. There have been many deaths including that of the Mayor. People are going missing, and even months of investigation have not been able to unravel even a single clue. Rufuz, our altar boy, our sheriff Richard, are also missing. We have no trace of them" said Father Mario.

The moment Father Mario uttered the name Richard, Rachel whispered, "Daddy" and looked at Grace. The gloom and desolation of a lonely young mother was apparent on Grace's face. The mother and daughter seemed to be holding on to a weak string of hope that Richard would be back with them some day.

"Last week, a fire devoured the west wing of the Church, and some items that are used during the holy mass have also gone missing. With deep concern, I would also like to tell you that we have noted some unusual happenings in the Church graveyard," continued Father Mario.

Amongst murmurs and whispers, he continued, "I must warn you for these are not good signs. It seems that an evil spirit has occupied our town. I want all of you to be careful and listen to me carefully, someone is practicing witchcraft."

Rumors of this evil were already being discussed in the city. Hearing it from Father Mario made people all the more uncomfortable and rather worried.

"I want all you to be careful. The cloud of darkness has surrounded us. Pray to the Almighty to protect this town from falling into the hands of the evil," said Father Mario in a grim voice.

"From tomorrow we will be starting day and night prayer and worship services for God's blessing and protection of this town. The Lord will not disappoint us and will shower his love on us," continued Fr. Mario as he made a sign of the cross.

Through the worry, there was still conviction in his voice. He knew his Lord would protect them from evil.

Loudly enough to be heard outside the church, Fr. Mario exclaimed, "Through the gospel and the power of the holy rosary, we will defeat the evil and save our home." Those in the church hall closed their eyes and joined hands as he uttered a brief prayer.

After a few minutes everyone except an old couple started to walk out of the Church. Rachel walked beside her mother and turned back to wave bye to Steve.

Chapter II

The Unseen World

Atop a hill on the outskirts of the city that same evening, Maya stood intently chanting some mantras. Her black kohl-layered eyes, long, flowing hair, and red gown were ravishing. Her chanting resonated through the surrounding forest. The sound became powerful, traveling further every minute.

Back at the church, Shirley and Joe had reached their silver car parked on the roadside. Maya's chanting reached them.

While sitting in the car, Shirley saw a wave of bright light. She noticed a lady's figure in front of the car but dismissed it as the reflection of the setting sun on her windshield. The wave of light entered her.

In the driver's seat, Joe closed his eyes from the light. A voice he did not expect made him look towards his right. Even though it was Shirley that he saw, she looked different, and it was not her voice he had heard and Shirley never wore kohl on her eyes!

The other church members made their ways home completely oblivious to the evil that was lurking in the silver car just steps away from their own parked vehicles.

Before he could ask Shirley about the kohl makeup on her eyes, he heard the strange voice again. This time it spoke in an unusual language. Shirley outstretched her right hand and Joe stared at it.

His body stiffened for a few seconds before he jerked in a strange manner. His eyes looked dilated. Suddenly, his body slackened and the expression on his face changed to one of peace and ease. It was as if he was under a spell. Shirley looked out of the window towards Father Mario standing at the entrance of the Church with the old couple.

Father Mario seemed to be praying for he had his hand on the lady's head. The sign of the cross was an indication for Shirley that the prayers had been completed. The old couple started to walk out of the Church. The old lady stopped and waved goodbye to Father Mario.

The sun was almost set. Father Mario's eyes glanced across the parking lot, seeing his people off when he caught a glance of Shirley and Joe parked across the road. He felt uneasy at the sight of them, and before he could pinpoint exactly what was making him uneasy, the silver car took off, swerving in his direction until it parked right next to him with a screech. He had always known Joe to be a safe driver and was a little surprised to see him being so rash. He walked up to the car to reprimand Joe and ask him to be safe, but his words never made it from his lips. The sight of Shirley smiling at him, her appearance and composure so changed, startled him into silence.

The old couple stopped to look back at what had caused the loud noises. All they saw was a glimpse of the door closing and the car driving past them hurriedly. The couple wondered where Father Mario had gone. They expected to see him at the gate, but he was no longer there.

Chapter III

Lust

Joe continued to drive the car at race-track speed. He even ran a red light and nearly ploughed over an old lady trying to cross the road.

Shirley was no longer sitting in the passenger seat. She was in the back seat with Father Mario who lay on the floor. Shirley had her feet on his chest. Every attempt made by Father Mario to rise failed. Shirley had immense strength for a woman of her stature… or even for a man.

Father Mario knew that his fears had come true. Shirley and Joe were in partnership with evil spirits. Either the couple had been taken over, body and soul, by evil entities, or they were willingly doing their bidding. Regardless of their circumstance, the couple was involved, and the town was in the hands of evil .

Suddenly the car stopped. Father Mario had no idea where he was. Father Mario heard a shutter open. He had barely managed to move from the floor to the seat when the car began pulling into the garage and the shutter came down. Within seconds the door on his side opened and Joe pulled at him roughly and lifted him on his shoulder.

Joe opened the back door of the house. Walking inside he marched straight towards the bedroom. All attempts made by Father Mario to free himself failed. Joe put him on the ground and tied his hands behind his back. Shirley followed them into the room.

Father Mario finally got a glimpse at Joe's face. The glazed-over expression and dilated pupils confirmed Father Mario's suspicions that Joe was possessed; he was under the control of evil spirits.

Joe came closer and lowered himself on Father Mario. "Enjoy my wife. Have fun! She's worked hard for you." After his teasing, he walked out of the room, locking Father Mario and Shirley in the small space together. Suddenly Father Mario's gaze fell on Shirley. She was busy undressing herself.

Father Mario had managed to sit on the bed, his hands still tied behind his back. He was flabbergasted. He shouted, "Stop, Shirley. Stop all this! What is wrong with you? You are husband and wife!"

Completely unmindful of Father Mario's voice, she moved in front of the mirror and picked up a bright red lipstick and started applying it.

Father Mario stood at the foot of the bed. He hurriedly tried to walk out the door, but she blocked his way. She gently pushed him again towards the bed.

He fell on the mattress and she lay very close to him.

She looked at him with eyes full of lust and started to move her hands on his chest.

Her touch irritated him, and he tried to shove her hand away.

Her hands reached his stomach and squeezed tightly. He twisted away in pain.

She allowed her hands to travel further down between his legs.

Father Mario shook his head and said, "You seem to be completely out of your mind Shirley," and again made an attempt to move away.

She continued with her seduction. Holding his shoulders, she tried to place her red painted lips on his.

Father Mario tried to put his arm on his face to prevent her from kissing him. With powerful hands she turned his face towards herself. Her lips moved from his lips, to his face, and then to his throat. Wherever her lips touched him, they left a bright red mark.

Shirley was completely in the hands of lust. She started to lick him. She bit his throat while rubbing his chest. She gazed deep in his eyes.

The hunger in her eyes offended him; after all he was a man of God! Father Mario closed his eyes. He couldn't stand her gaze. He knew he had to avoid looking in her eyes at any cost.

Shirley's hands were moving wildly in his hair. She pulled at it to bring his face close to hers and again tried to kiss him on the lips.

Father Mario shook his head wildly. All his attempts to break free from Shirley were going to waste.

Yes, she was possessed. She was possessed by the evil spirits just like Joe.

Shirley looked at Father Mario's body and suddenly disapproved of the white shirt covering his chest. She tore it apart and started kissing him on his bare chest and stomach. Once again her hands reached between his legs.

13

Father Mario managed to free his hands from the rope. He gripped his cross in his hands and said, "Shirley, I am your pastor. What happened to you? Why are you doing this to me?"

Shirley looked deep into Mario's eyes. She whispered, "Because I love you. I've wanted you for a long time."

Father Mario looked at her angrily. There was nothing he could do to bring her to her senses.

"I am a servant of the living God. Leave me alone."

"You sure pastor? Don't want these earthly pleasures?" said Shirley in a husky voice.

Mario held to his cross and started to pray. "No. I do not want. Please let me go," he replied.

Shirley laughed at Mario. He stared at Shirley in confusion. She stood up and moved to a chair. As she took a seat, Mario looked at Shirley, still unsure of her plan or motivation. She was silent. Taking a cigar from the table, she lit it and started to smoke.

Her seductive gaze never left Father Mario.

"What makes you think I don't know who you are? I wanted to give you a chance... a chance to join me... a chance to see the pleasures of life. Come join me," murmured Shirley.

"What? Join with you?" exclaimed Father Mario, quite in disbelief.

"Yes...I can give you everything. All the best things you can dream of. Tell me what you want..." saying this, Shirley got up and walked towards the dresser. She opened one of the drawers and dipped her hand into it taking out money and gold.

Throwing them at Father Mario, she said, "Money, gold, take anything that you want."

She pointed her hand towards the rosary around his neck and continued," Come. Let me liberate you. Throw those beads away!"

She walked towards the bed once again. The moment she reached it, she fell down on it. Shirley caught Father Mario's eyes stealing a glance at her jiggling breasts. She let out a moan full of desire and started to laugh.

Shirley unhooked her bra and threw at Father Mario's face moaning, "Come...You want these! Come and take them."

Suddenly, the room filled with a cool breeze. A fragrance of desire accompanied the breeze, and Father Mario started moving towards Shirley. With his gaze continuously fixed on Shirley, he started to pull the rosary from his neck. Suddenly Father Mario's eyes fell on his own image in the mirror. He saw himself pulling at the rosary beads. A light flashed from the beads and moved into his body.

Father Mario froze for a few seconds. Everything became clear to him. He knew he was under her influence and would have to be very strong to fight it.

Shirley looked at him confused.

He grasped the cross tightly and saw an image of Maya within Shirley. He could see Maya chanting away incessantly.

"I know who you are. You are Maya, the witch...You know I won't fall for your trap. You are using this innocent woman as a cover to seduce me...I know it is you, Maya." He said.

This angered Shirley. She knew she had to do something fast or she would lose him. All her efforts would go waste. She started to laugh loudly.

"You want me to be your slave so you can control the innocent people in this city and sabotage their lives forever. I always knew you were the one who was trying to ruin the church with your evil spells," continued Father Mario.

Shirley's laughter became hysterical.

In her own voice, Maya said, "I am sure you also knew my spell was the reason for the fire in the church and the dead bodies in the church yard."

"And... the grave openings and missing skeletons. You were behind those too,' said Father Mario who clung to the cross in his rosary.

"Yes, you're right. I wanted those skeletons for my rituals. They were necessary in order to please my deities and gain more power," spoke Maya's voice. "I worship those who want blood, who want human sacrifice. Their blessings make me powerful, make me ever living...make me the living goddess on earth," she continued.

Father Mario had only read about evil spirits. He knew they existed, but he never thought that he would encounter them.

"This city is my kingdom. The people belong to me. They now believe in me and in those who I worship. You are the only obstruction for me...The church bell rings only because of your presence. I don't want the presence of anything godly where I live," said Maya's voice looking straight into the eyes of Father Mario.

"Either you are with me, or you die... I want to give you the choice. If you join me, I will give you all the riches and pleasures of life. If not, a painful death...You decide," Maya bargained.

Father Mario was furious. The cool breeze soon changed to a stronger wind. The sound of chanting was audible throughout the room. It rang louder and louder.

Father Mario felt like dropping the cross and placing his hands on his ears, but he knew that he should hold tightly to what Godliness was left in the room. He looked towards Shirley and could clearly see Maya chanting mantras. He saw the open window and knew that it was his only chance to escape. He leapt up and jumped out of the window. When he hit the ground, he started to run in the direction of the church.

Maya stopped chanting and rushed towards the window. She saw Mario escaping her.

The door to the room opened and Joe entered. He came and stood close to Shirley and exclaimed, "He's gone!"

Shirley's face changed. She was in pain. Maya pulled out of her body, for she did not need it any longer. It had served its purpose. In a flash Maya jumped out of the window.

Mario ran through the street until he reached the church complex. He had to cross the graveyard before reaching the altar. Breathless, he continued to run through the graves. He found Maya standing near a grave, and he stopped. She started to walk towards him and said, "I gave you a choice between me and death... I see you've made your decision."

Mario looked at her.

Maya, with her inhuman strength, pulled out a broken cross from the grave. She raised it with her right hand and walked towards him. Mario still held the cross in his rosary with a firm hand. His fate was clear to him, and he accepted it. He closed his eyes and started to say his prayers.

She stabbed Mario in the chest with the sharp edge of the cross.

Father Mario fell to the ground with a cry.

Just before blood splattered all around, he uttered the name of God loud and clear for the last time in his life.

Still under Maya's spell, Shirley and Joe followed Maya to the grave. They witnessed Maya stabbing Mario with the cross. As she pushed it deep inside him, Shirley and Joe stared without emotion.

Chapter IV

Destiny

It is hard to believe that a morning can be dark. For the town of Bridgeport, even under a brightly shining sun, darkness loomed like a storm cloud. People were rushing out of their house and running towards the Church.

The site that they saw upon reaching the Church was gruesome. Hanging from the bells was Father Mario's dead body.

The crowd, mostly consisting of older people, looked in disbelief at the lifeless body. The old couple who was with Father Mario the previous evening whispered amongst themselves in disbelief. The lady could not bear it anymore. Holding her husband's hand she asked him to take her towards the stairs. With knees weak with shock and sorrow, she sat on the step by herself.

Rachel and Grace were also present in this crowd. Grace's brows cinched close to one another and the lines in her forehead creased deeply with concern.

Steve came running towards the bell closely followed by his parents. He stopped and cried aloud, "Uncle, uncle... what happened to you? Oh my God! Who did this?"

Steve's reaction was enough to ruffle the crowd. His mother reached for him. Squatting down to his level, she took Steve in her arms. Mother and son were completely broken at the sight of their dear pastor.

Grace clasped her hands and began to pray as tears rolled down her cheeks. Rachel left her mother's hand and ran towards Steve who was crying incessantly.

Rachel followed Steve's gaze in the direction to which Steve was pointing. Tears rolled down her cheeks. She pulled at Steve's T-shirt wanting him to look at the lollipop she was offering him.

Far away, the police siren could be heard. The people couldn't stand to continue being near the gruesome scene, and yet, they couldn't bear the thought of leaving—of abandoning Father Mario in such a state. After all it was about Father Mario, the man who had been with them through thick and thin, the man who had offered love and guidance during trying times. It was their turn to do the same for him and see their town through this evil, even if he was no longer with them.

Chapter V

Living Dead

Deep in the woods, just outside the city of Bridgeport, stood a lonely house. It was difficult to make out the house except for a ray of faint flickering light coming from one of its windows. The silence of the night was broken by occasional hooting of the owls. The crackling of dried leaves indicated that a predator of the night had just passed by probably in search of food.

Anyone moving closer to the house would easily make out that the faint light inside the house was coming from candles or oil lit lamps. Suddenly the complete surroundings started reverberating with the sound of chants. The complete environment around the house was eerie and vile. Even on a hot and humid night like today a chill could run down to the bones of even the strongest of persons.

Was there someone in this sinister house?

Yes, it was Maya standing near a wooden casket.

A shabby and a filthy looking man stood next to her shifting from one foot to the other. He would look at Maya and immediately look away avoiding making eye contact with her. This was Jerome, one of Maya's obedient servants.

Maya looked down at the casket. There was a body in the casket. A labored movement of the chest indicated that it was living. This was William who had been subjected to a dormant and a menacing life at Maya's hands.

Maya extended her hand to Jerome who eagerly opened a box nearby. The contents brought a smile to Jerome's face. Carefully, he pulled out a snake from the container and wrapped it around

Maya's hand. From inside the casket, William could hear the snake hissing. He prayed that the snake would pierce his body with its fangs. He wanted his pain to end. He had so little strength left from being entrapped in the casket for so many years. However, his feelings immediately changed to those of escape and revenge. He wanted to fight. He wanted to be free. He wanted to get back home.

By William's side, Maya came down to her knees, the snake still hissing around her hand. She brought her face close to William's and said, "I am going to drain you...drain you of your blood. That will make you weak and powerless."

William looked at Maya with a blank face.

"You will lie in this casket hungry and thirsty. You will have no strength to even open your eyes. You will cry in this darkness for centuries. But, no one will hear your cries...No one will save you."

William had lost count of the days he already had been in the casket. He had tried to put up a fight and flee so many times, but every time Maya's power overtook him, and he was back where he began—restless, worried, trapped. With every missed escape, the torture of his hunger and confinement grew.

Bringing the snake close to his face, Maya said, 'While lying here, alone and helpless, you will wish you had died. This is your punishment, William, my love that is the consequence for disobeying me, disrespecting me, and for rejecting my love."

He looked at her and let out a sigh. He knew fighting a snake with tied hands would not be easy. In the last few days, he had preferred death over life so many times. Every time he found he was alive, he wondered what destiny had in store for him.

"Say something, my sweetheart! You have nothing to say? Not even to me?" asked Maya. She wanted him to tell her about his pain and desire to die.

William shook his head. The tip of the snake's tail slightly touched him, and he felt a cold shiver run through his entire body.

Maya looked at him with disbelief and anger. She packed a punch at William's stomach. She was angry with him for not accepting her. He had refused to do as she wanted. Even days of torture had not made him relent.

She dug her nails into his body and William wriggled in pain. When he opened his mouth for a gasp of air, his tongue changed into a set of fangs.

Yes! He had the fangs of a snake.

The room was filled with her shrill and sinister laughter at the sight of William's fangs.

"Willie, my vampire. Why can't you just accept defeat and start obeying me? You're inviting pain into your life," said Maya as she moved closer to him.

"No one ever disrespects me...you understand?" said Maya and lowered the snake into the casket.

William saw the snake coming towards him. Before he could think of anything, the snake dug its fangs into his neck. He let out a cry of pain. Jerome watched from behind Maya with a blank face.

The snake sucked blood from William's throat and William breathed heavily.

With every passing second, the snake continued to drain him making William weak and pale.

Maya was enjoying what she saw.

Once done, the snake began to slither away from William.

Maya watched Jerome pick up the snake and place it back in the cage. She signaled him to put the casket back in the grave.

William who was alive was left to die in the grave.

Chapter VI

The Family

It had been quite a few years since Richard had gone missing, but there was not even a single day when Grace and little Rachel had not thought about him.

It was Grace's birthday today. Both of them were happy but the fact that Richard had left a vacuum in their lives could not be denied.

"Happy Birthday Mother!! Happy Birthday to you," sang out Rachel and entered the room. She had grown tall. While her nose was on her father, her eyes were exactly as Grace's.

Grace was sitting across the table in her wheel chair. She smiled back and extended her arms asking Rachel to hug her. They hugged and later Rachel helped Grace cut the cake. After enjoying some with Rachel, Grace maneuvered the wheelchair to face the wall where many photographs of them hung. These pictures meant much more to the family than simple records of past moments. The photos were the only way they could still see Richard.

Rachel came and stood next to her mother, and they exchanged a glance amongst themselves. "Rachel, what are you thinking, Baby?" her mother asked.

Rachel had made an effort to smile and taking a deep breath she replied, "Nothing Mother."

"I know you're thinking about your father" Grace said.

Rachel stopped forcing her happy expression and knelt down beside her mother and like a child, had placed her head in Grace's lap.

Grace smiled and stroked Rachel's hair. She'd bent down and kissed Rachel's forehead. She moved her hands towards Rachel's face and wiped the tears. Her heart went out to her daughter but there was nothing that she could do to ease her pain.

"Don't you miss Dad every minute?" Rachel had asked.

Grace had smiled and in a heavy voice replied, "Yes, baby."

"Is that why you haven't married since Dad died?" Rachel had asked wiping her tears with the back of her hand.

Grace looked at her daughter for a minute and then spoke. "Your dad was a good husband, a loving father, and a devoted Christian."

"We lost an honest-to-God good cop. He had too many commendations to even keep track of the number. He was next in line to become chief," had continued Grace. "But then all our dreams were taken away that day."

Every birthday and anniversary reminded her of him. Every happiness left her sadder!

Rachel had looked at the pictures on the wall. Eyes filled with tears she had thought about all those times when she had played with her father.

Seeing Rachel crying, Grace had also not been able to hold back her tears. "Mom, do you believe that Dad is really dead? Why would anyone kill such a nice person?" Rachel had asked.

"I don't know," Grace had replied.

"If he is dead, then what happened to his body?" Rachel had asked. Grace could not answer Rachel's questions. There was nothing she could tell her that would ease her sorrow. The answers would frighten her more.

"He could still be alive, couldn't he, Mom? I mean, if they never found the body... Right?" she had asked in a voice full of hope.

"I don't know, Baby. I don't know," Grace had said shaking her head. "I don't know what happened to him. I don't know where his body is hidden. I just don't."

They cried together comforting each other.

Chapter VII

Darkness

Maya stood on top of a mountain with her arms raised and hands outstretched in the air.

A teenage girl named Selina stood stark naked and chained to a tree in front of Maya. Maya's voice rang in the atmosphere. She was chanting mantras in an incomprehensible language.

Maya stopped chanting and walked up to Selina.

"I'm scared. I don't like this. You told me to just walk with you. Why have you chained me? Give me my clothes. Let me go!" pleaded Selina.

Maya's face reflected evil.

"Oh God! I want to see my parents. Let me go. Now! Please," continued Selina.

Without even looking at Selina, Maya extended her right hand and chanted more mantras. A sword appeared in her hand. Her voice grew louder.

All this was too much for Selina. She started crying hysterically.

"Oh God! Somebody save me. Please don't kill me," cried Selina.

Maya made a wild sound and angrily threw the sword at Selina.

The sword cut her throat, and blood splattered all around. Maya drew out a knife from her clothing and walked towards the girl. She dipped the knife in blood oozing out from Selina's throat.

She placed the knife on her hands, raised them towards the sky, and bowed her head in offering.

"Lehasha, my master, please accept the soul of this unblemished girl as my sacrificial offering to you. Please accept the prayers of this faithful servant of yours," said Maya in a reverent tone. From nowhere, the crow flew in and settled on the tree to which Selina was tied. It observed Maya.

Maya continued to hold the knife. Once again she chanted fervently. Her sound grew louder and louder. Her echoes came back to the place where she was standing. Slowly, she opened her eyes and said, "My Lord, please accept my prayers. Please appear to me so that I can confirm my prayers will be answered. Please show your true presence to me. Please give me a sign that I am following your rituals correctly. Show mercy on your servant, my Lord," prayed Maya with urgency.

Maya resumed chanting. The crow still watched. The sky grew suddenly overcast. Lightning struck the mountaintop. Unmoved, Maya continued chanting. The lightning reached Maya. The light was a bit too much for the crow. It began to blink its eyes.

The light took the shape of a man in a black robe. A long hood covered more than half of his face. The crow continued watching.

"I am appeased by your sacrifice" spoke Lehasha in a coarse voice. "Tell me, what do you want from me?" the evil Lord asked.

Maya was overwhelmed with joy. After all of her hard work and prayer, Lehasha answered. She had waited years for this.

Maya placed her knife back in her clothing and joined her hands.

"I am pleased at your rituals. Ask me. What is that you want from me?"

Maya was silent for a moment. All of these years, she had known what she wanted, but when the moment had come, she could not find words to express it. She bent down on her knees and bowed her head in front of Lehasha. Maya said, "Please give me the opportunity to become mother of your offspring."

Lehasha was silent for a few minutes. It wasn't often that he heard such a request from one of his disciples. "Ask only if you can fulfill the rituals that are written for my offspring's arrival," said Lehasha.

Maya remained on her knees. The only thing on her mind was getting Lehasha to say yes.

"It requires many years of preparation. My birth should take place in the town that worships me and prays for my arrival. That town should be completely under my control with no other godly places of worship. Each dark moon, the rituals must be completed at this place. A devout girl must be sacrificed in order to establish my authority and power. These virgin sacrifices will come back to life as my maids when I am reborn. When the time approaches for my arrival you will know. Things will reveal for themselves" ordered Lehasha.

Maya listened attentively.

The crow continued to listen from his perch on the treetop.

Selina lay on the ground drenched in blood. She was breathing heavily and it was only a matter of seconds that she took her last breath.

"What you ask for is not without consequences. If not done properly it will be a curse to you and cause painful death for you and your followers. Do you understand?" warned Lehasha.

"Yes, my Lord. I will surrender my life for your birth. I am willing to accept painful death if I fail in the duty that you give me. I am your servant, and I am at your mercy," said Maya.

She knew only one thing. She wanted to bear her masters child.

Lehasha took a look at Maya and said, "Your wish be fulfilled."

Gushing with thankfulness, Maya trilled, "My Lord, thank you for answering my prayers." She felt elated. Years of prayer and sacrifice paid off.

Lehasha again took the form of light before disappearing.

16 years later…….

Chapter VIII

Homecoming

On the state highway outside the city of Bridgeport, a car could be seen in the distance coming toward the town. It was a hot afternoon, and a crow sat watching the occasional car pass from atop the town's welcome sign.

As the car approached the crow, he honed in on the family inside. Steve drove while Laura sat next to him. In the back seat Amy read a picture book while Johnny napped.

The moment the car reached the welcome sign, Steve slowed and pointed at the board. Laura started to look at it through the windshield and smiled at Steve.

"Yes, here we are. Home, sweet home," said Steve. He looked back at the children and called out to Johnny, "Hey Johnny, wake up man. Look where we are now."

Johnny woke up and both children looked out of the window. They were excited to finally be in Bridgeport.

"This is where your dad grew up," trilled Laura .

Steve stopped the car immediately after passing the board. He stepped out of the car. Laura and children followed. Steve jogged down the open road a bit and extended his arms. He inhaled the country air he remembered from childhood. "Look Mommy! Daddy is so happy!" squeaked Amy.

"Of course he is… my angel. This was his dream. He waited for a long time to come back to this city," said Laura.

"Mommy, Daddy lived with grandpa and grandma here?" stuttered Johnny.

"Yes, baby. Then, they moved to New York," said Laura.

Steve admired the town from a distance. He motioned for the kids to come near him. Amy and Johnny ran to his side, and Laura followed.

Atop the welcome sign, the crow continued to watch over them without their knowledge.

Steve lifted Johnny and swung him in the air. "This is what I always told you. The smell of my city... can you smell it?" Steve asked.

The kids started to inhale.

"Nothing Daddy," stuttered Johnny before trying to smell again. This made Steve and Laura laugh.

"Yes. I smell flowers and trees," said Amy

"Yes, dear! This smell, the silence, the trees, the flowers, the butterflies... That is why your daddy wanted to come back here, back to where I lived with my parents and dearest uncle," said Steve in a jubilant voice. Finally he was back to the place where he belonged.

As Steve put Johnny back on the ground, Amy spoke up, "Uncle? Are we going to uncle's home? We have relatives here?"

Steve's face grew sad. Laura interjected, "No dear, we are going to our new home. Come on. Let's go. It's getting late,"

Motioning for the kids to follow her to the car; she took Steve by the hand and tugs him along with her.

The crow that was still sitting on the board let out a cry.

Once in the car, Johnny rolled the window down. Staring at the crow, he said to Laura, "Mommy, that crow makes loud noise."

They all looked at the bird.

Steve started the car and got it back on the road. He turned the radio on. The Bee Gees song, "How Deep Is Your Love," was playing. Looking at Laura, he started humming the song. Amy began reading her story book again while Johnny stared out of the window. Something caught Johnny's eye and he got to his knees in the car seat and tried to press his face against the rear windshield to get a better view.

"The crow," Johnny shouted.

To everybody's surprise the crow was following the car.

Amy dropped her story book and turned around.

"Forget it kids. It will go away eventually," said Laura and continued to look ahead while Steve drove toward their new house.

The crow increased its speed and landed on the hood of the car. Its talons gripped the windshield wiper and his beady eyes glared at the family inside.

Chapter IX

Final Adieu

It was a quaint morning. For years, Rachel was in the habit of pulling the curtains away from the window just before sleeping. She liked to rise to the morning sun falling on her bed, and today was no different. The early morning sun was trying to peep through Rachel's window and when the sunlight became strong enough she woke up. She looked at Grace who was sitting close to her in the wheelchair.

With her neck bent, Grace seemed to be in deep sleep.

The little kid in Rachel decided to play a prank on Grace. She quietly snuck out of the bed and, wanting to startle Grace, made a loud noise. Grace did not respond.

Rachel looked confused and worried. She had never known her mother to be in such sound sleep. She shook Grace to wake her up.

Grace's face fell to the side.

"Mom! Wake up, Mom! Wake up!" shouted Rachel as she shook her mother again. Rachel felt weak in the knees. She brought her finger close to Grace's nose. She couldn't feel Grace's breath.

Grace was dead.

Rachel was shocked and had no idea what she should do or how she should respond. She melted down to the floor crying hysterically and looking at her mother's dead body.

Helpless, confused, and worried, Rachel could do nothing but cry.

Towards the evening, it was time for Rachel to bid a final adieu to her mother. The two had a wonderfully close relationship. They were best friends, confidants through years of struggle and triumph.

The day of the funeral was not an easy time for Rachel. She stood close to the casket in which Grace's body lay. Tears dripping down her face, she looked at her mother lying lifeless. She bent down and touched her mother's face.

In the graveyard, neighbors and friends stood around them. They watched without any display of emotions or sympathy for Rachel.

Rachel drew out a rosary from her pocket and placed it on her mother's chest. She uttered a silent prayer, "Oh God, I give my mother to you--my only relative and only connection in this world. Like my Dad, I know I will never ever see her again. Oh God, please have mercy on my mother. In Jesus' name, I pray. Amen."

Rachel was a brave girl. She kissed her mother on the forehead and closed the casket. She looked at the people standing behind her. She suddenly realized that, amongst all these people, there was no one whom she could call her own.

Some of the people walked towards the casket in order to lower it into the freshly dug earth. Rachel put the first handful of soil on the casket and wiped her tears. People standing around started to cover the casket with the soil.

Near the grave, Rachel's life started to play in front of her eyes. She remembered her childhood. Her life was like a happy movie. She was perched on her fathers' shoulders while her mother walked by their side. They stood in line to buy some colorful balloons for her. Then, the scene changed to the time when she saw her father for the last time. Father Mario comforted them. Next, the memory of a homeless person robbing Grace and Rachel near the church flashed in her mind. When Grace had tried to run away, he followed and attacked them and tried to take her away. Rachel was reminded of how Grace lifted a rock and hit the assaulter on the face, and how he pulled at them both. During all the fighting Grace fell down and, by this time people walking out of the Church came to their help, Grace saw her mother was on the floor, in great pain and unable to move. She had felt helpless that day. Today she felt the same helplessness once again.

It was after this incident that Grace was limited to the wheelchair. Rachel remembered how her mother always knitted or embroidered things for her.

The grave was filled, and people started to leave. Rachel continued to stand next to the grave and cry. Rachel remained at the graveside all night. She stayed up very late crying, but eventually drifted to sleep.

When Rachel woke to the sunshine the next morning, Rachel looked around and realized that her mother was no more. Once again, tears started to flow down her cheeks. She stood up and, with labored steps, started to walk out of the graveyard.

Chapter X

The Wait

Surprisingly, the lonely house deep in the woods still stood strong even after years of abandonment. It was as lonely and sinister as it had been years before.

Jerome was outside the house sitting on a tree. He had a long beard, and it seemed that he had spent an eternity on the tree. He was eating some wild fruits.

A goat walked towards the house bleating. Jerome found the sound of the goat distracting and irritating. Jerome stepped down from the tree. He wasn't walking, but rather hopping like a monkey on all fours. He snuck towards the goat and tried to catch it. The goat jumped and ran far away from him. This angered Jerome. He followed the goat wanting it to catch it again at the next opportunity. He again jumped at the goat. The goat escaped, and Jerome fell on the ground.

This was more than enough for Jerome. He took some soil in hand and stood up on his feet. He uttered some mantras and threw the soil at the goat, cursing it.

Once again, he jumped at the goat. This time the poor thing lost the game, and Jerome picked it up in his arms. He started to walk back towards the house. Upon reaching the building, he tied the goat to a tree using the strong vines hanging down. The goat resumed bleating, but this time Jerome was happy.

He sat under the tree and looked at the sky.

Chapter XI

A Meeting

Steve and his family had settled in their new house. As a child, Steve had lived in Bridgeport, and he told Laura and the children so much about it that it was as if they had grown up there, too. In just two days, they already felt at home.

Laura was quick to arrange everything. On a shelf in the living room Steve had placed a beautiful picture of Jesus Christ. There were two handcrafted candle stands on both sides of the picture and the holy Bible in a red cover right in front of the picture. The house had already smelled of incense. Not a single day passed that Steve did not say his prayers.

In the evening, the family gathered in the living room for their prayers. Steve held the Bible close to his heart. Although Steve, Laura, and Amy sang a hymn reverently, Johnny was in a playful mood. Laura scolded him to join his hands and stand still.

Once the hymn was over, Steve placed the Bible back on the shelf and started saying his prayers. "God, your servant is back in this town to serve Your will. To reopen the church and bring the people back to you. Please empower me to become the light for these people who are living in darkness. I don't know what awaits me here, but I pray for the strength and power to do as you command me."

While Steve was still praying, a car stopped near the gate. They hardly knew anyone around and were not really expecting guests. Laura glanced at Steve. He didn't know who had arrived, either.

The doorbell rang, and Johnny ran towards the door, anxious to make friends.

When Johnny opened the door, there was a lady and a man standing at the doorstep.

It was Maya and Tony.

Laura had a burning candle in her hand when Maya stepped into the house without invitation. Suddenly the candle in Laura's hand blew out. "I'm Maya, and I live nearby."

"Hello. I'm Steve.'

Smiling, Maya extended her hand in greeting. Without breaking eye contact, she continued, "I am a tantric. This is my assistant Tony."

Steve shook hands with Tony and offered them a place to sit.

Steve noticed that Laura and Amy seemed uncomfortable. He also noticed that the candles in front of the statue had extinguished, and Amy was pointing this out to her mother. He saw that Laura was asking Amy to go and stand with her brother.

"I heard your family is new to the neighborhood," said Maya.

"Yes. We just moved in from New York," said Steve with a smile and a nod.

"That's nice."

An uncomfortable silence took over the room.

Maya looked around and, after some effort, said, "It is very rare that we have a new family in this town. I wanted to visit and welcome all of you to Bridgeport."

"That's very nice of you," replied Steve.

In order to make his guests comfortable Steve started to talk about their life in the city of New York.

"I was bored with the rushed life of the city--too much traffic all around and busy work schedules. I just wanted a normal life for my family. I heard the land is cheap here. It's nice to start off fresh in a small town like this."

Maya was looking at Steve and observing everything in the room carefully. "That's good to know," she said briefly before trying to look beyond closed doors. Her eyes fell on the statue which prompted a sarcastic smile on her face.

Suddenly, a loud and coarse sound of the crow echoed through the room.

"I think you have my pet here." Maya said with a smile.

This came as a surprise to Steve and his family because they were not aware of any animal in the house or outside. "Your pet?" asked Steve.

"Yes, the crow you have...that's my pet bird!"

Johnny ran out of the room through the back door. Steve, Maya, and everyone else followed. Johnny stood under the tree looking up at the crow.

The moment the crow saw Maya, it came and perched itself on her shoulder.

"Is the bird yours?" asked Steve.

"Ya... kind of," replied Maya

Johnny and Amy looked at the crow on Maya's shoulder with surprise. Maya started to pat the crow on its head.

"Ms. Maya, Are you going to take him home?" asked Johnny

She nodded yes, and the pout that formed on Johnny's face made her chuckle.

Steve started to walk back inside, and everyone followed him. The crow was still perched on Maya's shoulder.

Maya stood in front of the statue for a minute. Finally, she said, "It's a nice statue."

Amy, who had been closely watching Maya, said, "This is Mother Mary. We pray each morning and night to her." There was a tone of suspicion and disdain in Amy's explanation. Her sixth sense was on high alert, but she couldn't pinpoint what it was about Maya that made her feel so uneasy.

"You pray to the heavens every day?" asked Maya.

"Yes," replied Amy in a curt voice.

Maya continued to look at the statue and prayer books near it and said, "That is good to know."

Maya turned towards Laura. Their eyes met for a moment. Maya's glance made Laura feel uncomfortable. Suddenly, Laura could hear the sound of mantras chanted in Maya's voice all around her. The unwelcomed invasion into her home plus the eerie sounds made her edgy. She wasn't even sure if the others in the room could hear the chanting. Laura felt like all of her energy was seeping out of her.

"I do a meditation group at my center. I would like to invite you there. You could also meet others. Come and see if that interests you," said Maya.

Laura looked at Steve while he nodded at Maya.

"Uhh... I will come out one day," spoke Laura hesitantly for the first time since Maya had come to their house.

Maya did not care to look again at Laura and started to walk out through the main door. Tony followed.

Once Maya and Tony were out of the house, Steve closed the door.

The family could hear the squeal of Maya burning rubber as she sped away from their house.

Suddenly, the sound of something falling startled all four of them. When they looked in the direction of the noise, they noticed that the statue of Mother Mary had fallen from the shelf and broken into small pieces.

Steve ran towards the place where the statue had fallen and started picking up the fragments. Johnny and Amy bent down to help him.

Chapter XII

Rendezvous

Deep in the woods outside the city of Bridgeport, a group of hippies sat around a bonfire smoking weed and drinking. After a puff, the joint would find itself between the fingers of the next person.

While Ben, a middle-aged man who was already quite high, played the guitar and sang along, Tessa, a pretty girl not more than 30 years, and Ouso, who was far older than he acted, danced around the fire.

The group was reveled in their time together. They had everything they could want in those moments: joints, alcohol, firelight, music, and the safe cover of darkness. Another couple stood up and started to dance with Ouso and Tessa and the group applauded. Srini, another young hippie in the group, started to dance. He made an attempt at moon walking like Michael Jackson, and everyone started to laugh. The group was oblivious of the stranger creeping closer to them with every minute.

Rao had slowly started to move closer towards the group. He noticed that nearly all people in the group were high. One or two even seemed to be unconscious. Srini seemed to be dancing in a trance.

Rao stealthily moved in and joined the circle. Someone passed him a joint, and he took a deep puff before passing it on to the girl sitting next to him. With everyone in the group nearly unconscious, and himself under the effects of the weed, he felt confident in his plan. He walked towards Ben who was nearly unconscious. He lifted the guitar and started to play. Ben opened his eyes slightly at the sound of music and said, "That's great, Man. Awesome."

Rao nodded his head in thanks to Ben for the compliment.

Ben lifted his head once again. He made an effort and asked, "By the way, who are you?"

Before he received an answer, Ben lost his senses and started asking himself, "Who am I?"

Ben repeated the question to himself again and again. Someone passed a joint to him. He pulled at the joint while repeating to himself 'Who am I?'

Rao continued to play the guitar. He looked at Tessa. Even if his eyes travelled to other people they would come and stop at her. She was nearly unconscious and her head was lolling to the side.

"Oh, how beautiful she looks," thought Rao as he looked around. Nearly everyone in the group seemed to be falling asleep or unconscious. Some were on the ground while some were resting against each other. Rao looked at the moon and frowned.

Rao left the guitar and stood up. He started to walk away from the rest of the group.

It was a cool breeze that woke Ouso from his sleep. He looked at his watch and realized that it was 3:00 in the morning. He woke up the other members in the group. Trying to shake off the leftovers of last night's joint, Ben scrubbed his face with his hands and shook his head. He could faintly remember that they had company last night. He thought of asking others, but dismissed the idea. He searched for the guitar and found it lying nearby. Slowly all of them got ready to move on.

All of them started to walk deeper into the forest. Tessa walked behind Ouso. She was unaware that Rao was hiding behind a tree keeping a close watch on her.

Ben yawned and grumbled, '"Come on, guys. Move faster. I am still sleepy."

The group followed Ben through the woods and Rao followed them still hiding behind the dense trees. A beautiful blue bird with its chicks caught Tessa's attention. She came out of the group to take a closer look. Meanwhile the other members in the group moved ahead.

This was a good chance for Rao. He moved close to Tessa and covered her mouth. She tried to scream, but he had his hands firmly over her mouth. He was too strong to fight off. Rao lifted her and took her aside.

He dropped her on the ground. She was scared and shaking, but was able to see through the fear and recognize him from the guitar-playing last night.

Rao looked at her with hungry eyes. Suddenly, fangs appeared in his mouth. Tessa was terrified. She wanted to shout but her voice had escaped, unlike her body.

Rao kneeled next to her on the ground. He caressed her neck with his fingertips. Her soft skin excited him, and he pushed his fangs into her throat. Greedily, he sucked her blood.

Tears started to flow down her cheeks. She was in extreme pain. She wondered if anyone in the group had missed her.

She prayed for them to realize she was missing and return for her.

Unmindful of her absence, the group continued walking and reached an old bridge. Ouso stood to the side waiting for everyone to cross.

"Careful and walk straight," he said to one of the girls in the group.

As the members started to cross the bridge one by one, Ouso realized that Tessa was not with them.

"Tessa, Tess? Where are you?" he shouted. When there was no reply he ran back down the trail to search for her.

Ben and the other group members followed. A chorus of voices called out for Tessa.

Rao still had his fangs in Tessa's throat.

Ouso reached the spot. He noticed some movement behind the bushes. Springing towards the rustling leaves, Ouso saw Tessa on the ground and Rao next to her. He grabbed at Rao's shoulders and tried to throw him off of Tessa, but Rao was too strong.

"Who are you?"

Rao raised his head. It was a horrible scene. Tessa lay on the ground helpless. There was blood dripping from his mouth and a snarl distorted his features. Ouso's presence angered Rao. He moved his head wildly and roared like a lion. All this scared Ouso. He withdrew his hand from Rao's shoulder and stepped back. All he could do was utter, "Oh God!"

Rao started to take heavy steps towards Ouso. Each step was a heartbeat in Rao's chest, and with each heartbeat, Tessa's blood strengthened him even more. By the time Rao reached Ouso, he was already on his knees and pleading, "Please, please. Don't kill me. Please." He didn't even have the courage to look at Rao. "I'm sorry. I shouldn't have come here," he continued.

Rao pierced Ouso with an angry stare. He had been disturbed. It was not often that he got to drink blood from such a beautiful throat. Her peachy complexion made her look all the more desirable. He had to work hard to get it. He wiped his mouth with his sleeve and started to walk away.

Ouso dropped to the ground. He had no words to explain how he was feeling. He had just been saved. Suddenly, he heard Tessa's pained voice. He stood up and hurried towards her. "Oh my God! What was that creature?" he cried as he helped her stand up.

Tessa raised her hand to her throat and wrenched in pain.

"You ok?" asked Ouso.

Tessa was barely able to shake her head. She tried to take a step with Ouso's support, but was too weak for that. She was still losing blood from her wounds and was in shock.

Ouso took off his t-shirt and wrapped it around her neck. He lifted her on his back and hurried as quickly as he could.

Chapter XIII

A Lonely Retreat

The clock read 12 midnight. The calendar lying on the table had the day's date beautifully highlighted. In Rachel's handwriting was written, "Mom's Birthday."

A balloon on the wall burst loudly, but Rachel sat still next to her mother's wheelchair. Another balloon burst. Rachel slowly turned her face in the direction from which the sound came. Her eyes fell on Grace's photograph on the wall. She again looked at the wheelchair. She had cried so much since yesterday that now tears refused to drop from her eyes.

Just next to her lay a box gift wrapped with a beautiful red bow. Rachel lifted the box and placed it on the wheel chair. She softly moved her hand on the wheel chair as if caressing her mother.

She visualized herself wishing her mother and giving her the gift. She pecked a kiss on her mother's forehead.

Realizing the reality, Grace's absence in her life, she once again started crying uncontrollably. She dropped her head on the wheel chair as she had placed her head on her mother's lap so often before she passed.

Instead of the softness of her mother, Rachel felt cold leather. "Mom, I miss you. I miss you so much. First it was Daddy and now you...How can you both leave me alone and go away?" said Rachel amidst her tears. She moved the wheelchair as if shaking Grace.

She looked at the wheelchair and said, 'I feel alone. Who is there for me? I have nobody to even speak to. It is hard for me to pass each day. I miss you so much, mom," she sobbed, as if her mother could hear everything.

Rachel noticed a piece of paper fall from the hand rest of the wheelchair and onto the floor. Rachel lifted the paper and looked at it. It was a hand drawn sketch of a woman. The woman had a glittering ball of light in one hand, and the other hand was placed over the ball. Below the picture were the words, "Maya's Paradise."

Rachel had no idea who the lady in the sketch was or where the paper had been until then

For a second, she felt her mother's hand caressing her head. Rachel could feel her presence in the room, very close to her as if Grace was trying to communicate something to her. She looked at the hand-rest almost expecting more notes.

She took the note and moved to stand near the window. "Mother, what does that mean? Why did you keep this here? What is it that you want to tell me?" murmured Rachel.

She stared at the picture some more and wondered who Maya was and where her paradise was.

Chapter XIV

A Vampire Strikes

In her house, Maya sat in front of the magic ball. The lights reflecting out from the ball made it look attractive, not like the dangerous tool of evil it truly was. Tony was standing just behind her. The chanting of mantras could be heard in her voice. A small group of people sat around her in a circle holding each other's hands. Laura was among the attendees.

Just next to Laura sat Sandra. Maya saw something in her ball and looked at Tony as if signaling him. He left the room.

Ouso and Ben walked into Maya's paradise. Tessa was on Ben's back. They met Tony at the door. Without any words, Tony led them to the room where Maya and the group were chanting.

Ouso motioned Ben to be quiet. Once the chanting was complete, Maya opened her eyes and saw them standing in the doorway. She noticed Tessa, who was only partially conscious. She signaled the group to leave. Sandra and Laura walked out of the room together.

Just outside Maya's paradise, Laura and Sandra stood for a small chat. "Don't forget about the dance program I mentioned, said Laura.

"We'll meet again next week. Say my "Hi" to the kids," said Sandra.

Laura smiled back and said, "Sure," before they started to walk in different directions.

Inside, Maya bent down and noticed the teeth marks on Tessa's throat. She looked at Tony and smiled.

"A vampire in Bridgeport?" said Maya

Ben's jaw dropped. He had no idea what Maya was talking about. Ouso shook his head in disbelief and exclaimed, "You're right! He is a vampire! When I saw him, he had long fangs and his face was covered in blood!"

"It hurts!" Tessa broke in with a moan. "He caught me and pushed me on the ground. He thrust something sharp in my throat," ok Tessa choked.

An uncomfortable silence took over the room. Maya once again looked at Tessa. She tried to touch Tessa's wound, but the poor girl writhed in pain.

"He fed on my disciple. He will not go unpunished. They seem to have forgotten their friend," uttered Maya. She was flushed with anger at this point. She could not let this go.

Ben, Ouso, and Tessa exchanged glances. They knew what Maya was saying was true, but still it was very hard to believe everything that was happening around them.

"Call your guys. There will be another gathering next week. Same place," said Maya in a strong voice.

"We normally meet once a month," interrupted Ben.

"The vampire can't go loose in our territory!" fumed Maya.

"We need to capture him before he attacks others, or worse, another one of my disciples," said Tony.

The three of them were too shocked and too scared to say anything.

Ouso gathered his courage and said, "Ok. I will call all of them."

Maya quickly started giving instructions to all four of them. "Do not tell anyone about the attack. I don't want to cause panic. We want this town to come to us for help, after all."

Ouso, Ben, and Tony shook their heads. Maya brought her ball of light right above Tessa and started chanting mantras again. A light emanated from the ball and fell on Tessa. Once she was finished with the ritual, Tony wrapped a white piece of cloth around Tessa's neck. Without opening her eyes, she said to Tessa, "You will shortly feel better."

Tessa felt confident after Maya's ritual. She stood up on her feet, though she was holding on to Ouso all the while.

"You can go now, "said Maya.

The three of them started to walk out of the room. The cat was still in the room. It jumped on a cage lying next to the door. The white snake in the cage started hissing. Ouso got distracted and bumped into a tall statue lying nearby. He held the statue in order to stop it from falling. The three quickly rushed out of the room. Once the three left, Maya paced the room restlessly.

"A vampire in my territory! It is the first time in probably...16 years," said Maya.

"16 years?" asked Tony

Maya shook her head.

"Those vampires once learned a hard lesson. They've never wanted to fight with me since. Not after I chained William.

Never even bothered to enter this city!" said Maya still walking around frantically.

"The treaty that vampires need your permission to enter Bridgeport is still active, right?" asked Tony.

"Yes, it still applies."

"Then how and why did this vampire come here?" continued Tony.

"I don't know. Let's find the blood sucker and ask," fumed Maya.

Tony nodded his head obediently. Maya looked around the room. Something was making her uncomfortable.

"If he is bold enough to enter my territory, that is not a good sign," said Maya.

Tony looked at her with surprise and asked "What purpose could he have here?"

"We will find out soon," said Maya with a wicked smile on her face.

The cat walked closer to Maya and made a loud sound. Maya let out a loud laugh. She knelt down and, taking the cat in her hands, started petting it.

Chapter XV

A Weekly Meal

Out in the deep woods, Jerome sat under a tree humming a tune to himself. He was still looking at the sky. The goat lay near him held down by the tree roots around its feet. The sky looked beautiful with the stars shining brightly.

Jerome stood up. He stretched his entire body and made a wild sound. Picking up the goat, Jerome walked deeper into the woods all the while humming the same tune. He stopped and looked around. He pulled the goat closer to his face. The goat let out a bleat and he caressed it to quiet it.

He turned and climbed the stairs of the verandah. He pushed at one of the windows and threw the goat inside. He climbed in after the animal. With the commotion from Jerome and the goat, the birds that had made the house their home started flying around. He picked up the goat from the floor and moved further inside the house. He started to talk in an unearthly language. It seemed as if he was calling out to someone.

Shouting, "Handambaraha...Hamdo Hamdo...Hamdo," Jerome came to stand before a locked door.

There were thick chains that had been interwoven around the handles and big metallic locks had been applied. Just above the door was a picture of a double headed snake. Jerome placed the goat on the floor. With his right hand on the lock, he pressed the index finger of his left hand into a sharp edge on the side of the door. Blood dripped from his finger. He touched the blood-stained finger on the fangs of the snake. The blood seemed to dry immediately. The door opened with a loud noise.

Jerome picked up the goat once again and entered the room. He moved towards a lamp sitting on the table and lit it.

Jerome again shouted,"Handambaraha...Hamdo Hamdo...Hamdo."

He came to stand in front of a statue with a sword. Jerome touched the sword with his right hand and placed his forehead on it. The concrete floor towards one side of the room started giving way. A flight of stairs appeared. He picked up the lamp and started walking down the stairs.

When Jerome reached the basement, the light from the lamp he held fell on a casket lying on the floor. He once again uttered his mantra, "Handambaraha...Hamdo." He could sense the struggle-filled movements coming from the casket even in the dark. The scraping and shaking sounds of wood against wood made an eerie concert of echoes in the otherwise empty room.

Jerome lifted the cover of the casket. A peculiar odor spread in the room. William, who was still chained to big and heavy wooden bars in the casket, was thrashing around to escape.

William was pale, tired, and helpless. There was desperation in his eyes. He tried to outstretch his hands towards the goat, but failed for his hands were in chains. His hunger was nearly tangible. The years in isolation and restraint had truly damaged him.

Jerome brought the goat closer to the casket, and fangs appeared in William's mouth.

When the goat was finally within reach, William struck his fangs into the goat's throat and sucked its blood. The goat let out a cry and tried to escape. As time passed, the goat stopped fighting. It had accepted its fate rather than met its fate. Jerome held on to the goat tightly for William, who sucked its blood to the last drop. Once William was done, he let out a loud cry.

Jerome dropped the goat on the floor and looked at William. William smiled through his blood-stained face.

"Rufus afaso histimal tunako," muttered Jerome as he raised seven fingers. He planned to return with more blood in seven days.

William looked at Jerome with pleading eyes.

Hast... Hala...Hamdo," muttered Jerome once again and spat at William.

Jerome started to close the door of the casket. William let out a mewling whimper as if pleading for mercy and, once he was sure that he could not get anything more from Jerome, he let out a loud cry and started moving in the casket frantically.

Jerome scooped the dead animal from beside the casket and walked back up the stairs. In front of the statue once again, Jerome touched his forehead on the sword, and the concrete floor came back to its place. He jumped out of the window, closed it, and started to walk away from the house.

While walking away, Jerome heard the howl of a fox. Far away he could make out its glittering eyes. Jerome threw the dead goat on the ground. In a few seconds, the fox emerged and started feeding on the goat. Satisfied, the fox howled. Jerome went on his way through the woods.

Chapter XVI

The Search

Rao was wandering in the forest. Suddenly, a particular odor caught his attention and he started to smell around. With every sniff, his movements became more hurried. In spite of darkness all around him, he knew where he wanted to go.

He again sniffed hard and smiled. He could recognize the smell. "William, William," said Rao to himself.

He could not believe that he had been able to find William after so many years. After reigning in his excitement, Rao heard a humming sound. He looked around, but he could not see anyone. Rao started walking toward the humming sound. He darted from one tree to another, taking care not to be seen by this unknown person.

Rao finally got a glimpse of Jerome walking aimlessly in the woods. He was still humming. Rao again sniffed hard and knew that this man had been around William.

Rao emerged from behind a tree and stood in Jerome's way. There was no point waiting anymore. After all, answers were sought.

Jerome stopped, startled. He had never seen a person in these woods at night before.

Rao took a few steps towards Jerome and said, "William."

This was more than enough to scare Jerome.

Rao opened his mouth. His fangs moved swiveled violently.

Jerome turned and started running through the jungle. To gain an advantage, he chanted mantras that would aid in his escape.

Jerome continued to run through the forest. Rao caught up with him and punched him in the face. Before Jerome could do anything, Rao lifted him up in the air.

Without putting him down, Rao asked Jerome, "Where is William?"

Jerome shook his head. Rao put Jerome back on the ground, but maintained his near-deadly grip around Jerome's neck. His voice roared, "I asked you, where is William?"

Back at the center, Maya had been standing at the altar with a book in her hands. When Jerome's voice began chanting mantras in her head, it startled her. She knew he would only do such a thing if he were in trouble. Concerned, she moved closer to her ball and watched everything play out between Rao and Jerome.

Rao started to smell Jerome's hair and face.

"Don't lie to me. I can smell him. I know you have been around him. I can feel his presence," raved Rao.

Jerome did not reply.

In a fit of rage, Rao began beating Jerome.

Jerome cried out in pain. His face was covered in blood.

"William is my maker. I know he is in captivity someplace nearby," he shouted as another hit landed upon Jerome's jaw.

"I want him back. I want to take him back to our world," shouted Rao. He seemed to be driven by a deep seated motive.

Jerome was surprised and terrified. Rao was much more powerful than him. Feeling terrified he closed his eyes and started to chant and cry.

"Open your eyes! Look in my eyes when I'm speaking to you!" screamed Rao in an unwavering voice.

"Tell me where my maker is or you will die right now," said Rao clenching his teeth. He continued to stare at Jerome. Even though his presence was overwhelming Jerome did not relent. Rao had tried everything--pain, threats, persuasion--but Jerome did not relent. He lost his patience and stepped closer to Jerome to bite him. His fangs appeared, and he bent over to strike.

The moment Rao's fangs touched Jerome's skin, the snake symbol on his throat started to glow. It suddenly became red hot. It emitted light that fell on Rao's face, and Rao immediately felt his skin burning. Rao jumped back and looked at Jerome.

Jerome felt relieved to be free from Rao's strong grip. He was also grateful his mantras had finally kicked in.

While Rao writhed in pain, holding his face and whining for it to stop, Jerome availed the opportunity and ran away from Rao.

Jerome's escape infuriated Rao, so he started throwing anything and everything that he could get his hands on towards Jerome.

Maya saw Jerome running away; she smiled and waved her hand on the ball.

The images vanished.

Chapter XVII

A Trip in the Past

The sun started to slide down the sky and evening set in.

Rachel walked towards the church. She had a large packet in her hands. As she approached the church, she sighed at the unkempt state it was in. Unclean and untidy, the wild grass had not been cut for months. She was reminded of the day when Father Mario was found dead on the church bell. How beautiful the church and the path looked at that time despite the horrible event. She walked on the path and reached the porch.

To her surprise, the main door of the church was open. It had been years since the doors had been opened. She stood at the door step considering all the memories she had in this place. She hesitated to enter the prayer hall. Like a small child, she peeped in to assuage her fears and bad memories. Rachel noticed that there were few cobwebs and the statues gleamed like they always did years back. The air smelled fresh. Someone had just cleaned up the whole place. She took a few apprehensive steps towards the altar and saw a person already kneeling down on the pew praying.

Rachel quietly sat down on the pew. With only the back of the person praying visible, her nerves and imagination took over. It was unusual to have strangers in her small town, and his presence did anything but calm her. She closed her eyes to pray, but her entire attention was on the man praying at the altar.

She eventually let her guard down enough to begin her prayers, but when the person at the altar rose, Rachel startled and opened her eyes. She saw the person at the altar walk towards a table to light candles. He smiled at her. The rosary around her neck caught his attention. He opened the Bible and started to read out a passage aloud. He read the entire passage, reverently closed the Bible, and made a sign of the cross.

Rachel was at ease by now even though they still had not been introduced. She closed her eyes and resumed her prayers. She was in the presence of a holy man. It had been years since prayers had taken place in the church. Rachel was thankful he had come.

When Rachel opened her eyes, the man was standing near her. They looked at each other and continued to smile.

"I'm Steve, the new pastor. We bought this church."

Rachel again smiled. The news made her happy. She, and most of the Christians left in town, had lost all hope of the church reopening. She was thankful that a pure, God-fearing soul came to the city to revitalize their faith.

"Hi. I'm Rachel. I live nearby," replied Rachel.

They both went silent for a minute.

"It's great to know that our church is starting again," continued Rachel.

"Yes. My uncle was the last pastor in this church, like 14 years ago. After he was killed no pastor was willing to come here for service," said Steve.

Rachel looked closely at Steve for a moment. Suddenly, many memories started to play in front of her eyes. She remembered the boy who was crying at the dead body of Mario.

"Steve... Wow. The small Steve who always wore white shoes to school?" exclaimed Rachel.

Steve looked back at her with surprise. "Yes, that's me and you?

"I'm Rachel. We studied in the same school," she said nearly shouting. He reminded her of everything nice and bright in her childhood.

"Rachel. I remember you now. You haven't changed much," said Steve.

They both hugged each other. Stepping back from Rachael's arms, Steve held out the candles he wanted to light.

"Sure. Let's do this together," said Rachael and walked behind Steve towards the wall.

It didn't take them long to open their hearts to each other.

"After my uncle was killed, my parents were too scared to live here. They felt that the town was haunted. They wanted to go as far away as possible. My dad got a job in New York," said Steve lighting a few candles.

"I studied in New York, went to the seminary. Just like my uncle who was my mentor and the reason for my becoming a pastor," continued Steve.

"My wife and I, with our two children, hoped for a day to come back to this city where I was born. I heard this church was closed down and no pastor was willing to come and take over. I heard the city is full of crime and evil worship," said Steve looking at Rachel.

"True," replied Rachel looking straight into Steve's eyes.

"With my savings and from donations from our church members in New York, I was able to open the church doors again," said Steve taking a deep sigh.

Rachel took a few candles from Steve's hands and started placing them on the wall.

"That's so great Steve. Sorry, Pastor Steve. Your uncle loved this city. My mom always spoke so highly of Father Mario. She prayed for his soul. We often came to church every year on the anniversary of his death to pray near that bell for him," said Rachel. Her voice had grown heavy while talking about her mother and Father Mario.

"You remember today is the day when Father Mario was killed?" spoke Rachel.

Steve nodded his head in reply and continued putting the candles on the wall.

"I know. I lit the candles today in his memory. I want him to see from the heavens the light in this church so he will know that his nephew is back in this city to continue his great work of serving the Lord and helping the needy."

Rachel looked at the long line of candles which they had already posted. She then looked at Steve as if she wanted to say something important to him.

"Pastor, I just want to warn you. This city is not what you think it is. It has changed a lot since you left. Today there is no peace, love, or harmony. Nobody loves or cares for anybody else. Most families, like your parents, left this town long ago. Now it is full of hippies, drug addicts, and evil-worshippers. In short, darkness has taken over this city. I don't know what it is, but there is nothing good here any longer."

Steve smiled back at Rachel in a reassuring manner and said, "I know. I heard about it and have noticed it myself. That's why I haven't disclosed to anyone but you that I am the new Pastor or that I came here to open the church. I want to find out what the real problem is before we publically open the church and start the prayers."

Both kept quiet for a few seconds.

"I'm organizing a carnival in this town hoping the people may come by. Maybe we can rebuild that connection and friendship among neighbors," said Steve.

"Our church group from other cities will volunteer for the carnival. They'll see if there are any people in this town who are religious and would like to join the church. Additionally, I plan to prepare a census of the people in the city since there is no city office to get neighborhood information," continued Steve.

Rachel was deep in her thoughts causing the lines on her forehead to deepen. She was worried about something.

It was not long before she spoke. "I just wanted to remind you. Whoever killed your uncle may be still in this city. If they find out who you are, it won't be good. I'm worried."

Steve smiled back at her. He was confident in himself, and he was confident of the Almighty's grace on him. He knew the path that he traveled was tough, but was confident of his destination.

"Please, please warn your wife and children to be always alert and careful," beseeched Rachel.

"Yes, I will," replied Steve.

During their conversation, they had made their way outside to the church bell. They looked up at it for a few minutes. Rachel took a few steps towards the bell and started ringing it. Steve folded his hands in prayer.

Years had passed since the bell was rung. The church looked beautiful with candles all around.

Chapter XVIII

The Hunt

On another dark night in the middle of the woods, the group of hippies sat laughing and smoking around their bonfire. No moon shone, and the light of the bonfire didn't extend very far into the darkness. A young skinny boy with a scarf around his waist was dancing while Ben was playing guitar.

Like before, Rao was watching from behind a tree. He looked tired and exhausted. There were burn marks on his face. He moved to another tree in order to get a better view of the group which had stolen away his prey once already.

Tessa and Tony sat side by side. On the other side of Tessa sat Maya with more than half her face covered with a scarf. Srini passed her joint to Maya who took it and passed it to Tony, who took a puff and passed it to Tessa. The bonfire flared.

Rao touched the burn marks Jerome had inflicted on his face. His eyes were fixed on Tessa.

A fox howled far away as if warning that there was a predator far greater than himself lurking nearby.

Most of the members were too high to notice. They were all sprawled on the ground, content and oblivious.

After some while, Ouso got up and started calling out to the others, "Come on, guys. It's time to leave." He pulled at Srini.

Srini broke free from Ouso and again sat on the ground. "Oh come on. It's so early," she said.

Ouso continued shouting at the other members and kept shaking them. Finally, he succeeded in having everybody up. He then set them moving. He moved a little closer to Maya, but she motioned him to leave.

Everyone except Maya and Tony left the campsite. They continued to sit around the fire. Maya took a few deep breaths in an attempt to catch Rao's smell, but she couldn't smell anyone. Her eyes darted from one direction to another.

Rao still had his eyes fixed on Tessa. The thought of jutting his fangs into her delicate neck was giving him a high. He saw that Tessa was the last person in the group. At the next opportunity, he grabbed her and pulled her to the side.

His rapid movements wafted his sent Maya's way, and she caught his smell. She signaled to Tony, who ran in the direction in which Rao was about to relish Tessa's blood.

Tessa lay on the ground frozen in fear. This time she knew what Rao had in store for her. She started to cry and plead. Rao bent down over her and held her from her throat. She tried to push him away, but he was too strong for her. He bent over to bite her throat.

Suddenly a silver mesh covered his face. He felt a burning sensation on his face. Writhing in pain, he withdrew his hands from Tessa's neck to free himself from the net.

Tessa shrieked and started to run away. She was more than relived to see Maya come to her rescue.

Maya planted her feet firmly on the ground. She held to the net tightly.

Rao tried to break free from her grip, but she had more power than him. His every attempt to break from the net burned his skin all the more.

Ouso stood behind a tree watching all that was happening. Tessa ran up to him and they hugged.

"Who are you?" growled Rao through the searing threads of the net. He again tried to push Maya away. Her foot got stuck in a fallen tree and she lost her balance. She fell on the ground giving him enough time to pull off the silver mesh from his face and threw it aside.

When Maya fell to the ground, Tony stepped in. Brandishing a sword, he started to walk towards Rao. They fought.

Rao was much stronger than Tony and was able to overpower him.

Maya recited her chants loudly. She outstretched her hand. Water poured on her hand from an invisible bowl. She threw this water at Rao, who immediately began to weaken. He collapsed to the ground, unable to fight.

This was a good opportunity for Tony. He rushed up to Rao with a rope in his hands and tied Rao to a tree. Once he was sure that Rao was securely tied, he picked up the sword and handed it to Maya.

Maya let out a shrill laugh. She circled the tree and mocked, "'The vampire in search of his maker!" She placed the sword on Rao's throat.

"Who are you?" asked Rao.

Maya let out a laugh and said, "Welcome to Maya's Paradise."

Rao was confused. "You are Maya... the Witch?" he asked.

"Yes, I am. I am Maya the witch," she shouted.

"I'm sure you've heard about me. Haven't you? I'm the witch who loved your maker, William." Her voice rang in the otherwise dead-silent forest.

"You call it love? You wanted a slave, not a lover. When my maker refused to obey your orders you destroyed him and made him captive," replied Rao. The initial fear had settled. He was prepared for the ultimate fight. What pained him was the thought that he might not be able to free William.

"William will never be your puppet! Unlike some mortals here,"" spat Rao in Tony's direction.

"So you have heard all of the stories. Yes, William is carrying out his punishment. I don't take kindly to my lovers disrespecting me. You care to join him?"

Rao kept silent.

"And this mortal will become very powerful soon," said Maya pointing towards Tony.

"Stronger than William ever was. I gave William more than enough time to repent because I loved him. But not anymore. Your maker's days are numbered. He will die soon," she continued.

"But not before you," she said holding the sword high in the air.

"You can kill me, witch. I will die for my maker," roared Rao. He stared Maya in the eyes, unshaken by her power or the fear of death. "But remember somebody more powerful than me will come and defeat you. It is only a matter of time. You don't know the power of vampires," continued Rao.

Maya cackled. "The power of vampires? That is very funny! Okay, I will wait, but as I said, not for long. William has just a few more days left anyway," said Maya still laughing.

"And feast your eyes on true power," roared Maya. She swung the sword with all her strength and pushed it through his heart.

In the distance, Ouso and Tessa huddled behind a tree to listen to the commotion. Tessa closed her eyes, but felt no safer. They could hear Maya laughing evilly and the gory slice of flesh as she plunged the sword through Rao.

With a large smile across her face, Maya regarded the place where Rao was tied. There was nothing more than a pool of blood. His body was gone.

Maya threw the sword towards Tony, who caught it. She started to walk through the woods with Tony following her closely.

Chapter XIX

Paradise

Every time Rachel went out of the house, it was with a hidden objective. Wherever she went, she looked around for Maya's Paradise. She still had the sketch that she found on her mother's chair. She knew that her mother was trying to communicate with her through this. She had the sketch imprinted in her mind.

Inside Maya's Paradise, Maya sat near the crystal ball. While Tony was on his knees, she circled her hands over it. Nearby, a group of women of different ages sat in a circle holding hands. Smoke rose from a jar kept next to the ball, and the room was illuminated by the light from the crystal orb. Maya lifted the jar of smoke in her hands and blew hard into it. The smoke rose higher.

Maya raised her right hand and chanted some mantras. Continuing with her chanting, she placed her hand on her chest. Tony took the jar of smoke from Maya and began to move it around the group.

Maya's chanting grew louder and faster. All members in the group closed their eyes.

"Let the power of the universe fill this room," chanted Maya. The group repeated the same behind her.

"Let the power of light and darkness fill this room. Let the power that can control fill this room," she continued. Once again the group repeated the line behind her.

Tony circled the group a few more times before kneeling down on the floor near Maya who, once again, blew hard in the jar making the smoke rise. The light emitting from the jar increased.

Tony held on to Maya's left hand while Tessa the other. A sudden wave of energy started to flow amongst the members present. All of them felt an unseen energy. Maya's voice continued to ring in the room, and the group repeated the chants behind her.

"Enlighten us, Oh, Lord! We are sick of this world. Let our eyes be open now. Show us our future with you," chanted Maya in a loud and clear voice.

"Oh, Lord Lehasha, Show us the Promised Land that is waiting for us. Show us our life there," continued Maya. The group continued to repeat the chant.

Suddenly, Maya's face changed. There was a strange kind of wildness on her face.

"Ashey, Ishiha, Lahate. Swahe Ashey, Ishiha, Lahate. Swahe," was heard. With every chant, her voice grew louder and louder. It was as if the room reverberated with her chanting.

All of the members sitting in the circle began to shake. The energy seemed to be travelling faster through them. The light emanating from the ball brightened. The room filled with light, smoke, and Maya's voice. The candles in the room flickered, and wind started to blow in the room. Maya looked possessed. A blue light reflected on the faces of each of the members. The members were entranced.

Laura smiled. Like the others, she was in a trance. She felt that she was weightless and flying through the clouds like a bird. She could see all the members sitting on the floor. She felt she was moving through the stars and passed close to the moon. A beautiful, bright light caught her attention; floating towards it, she saw an open space that was beautiful, lush, and green. She noticed that all of the group members were standing in this verdant meadow. She was pleased to see them there.

In the meadow was a big gate. The gate to paradise! Sandra was happy to see Laura reach the gate. Laura walked up to her, and they once again held hands. The two of them started to walk towards the gate.

A guard opened the gate for the two of them. The moment they placed their first step inside the gate, their clothes changed to green leaves. Inside the gate was a green luscious garden with lots of fruit trees. The trees were loaded with fruits.

The two friends ventured around the garden. The other members also wandered around. Some of them were chasing butterflies while others chased bubbles and shook tree branches for fruits. Musicians were scattered all around the garden. Sandra and Laura looked at each other and smiled. They were having a nice time together and continued to meander.

They reached an apple tree and saw some apples scattered on the ground. They noticed a white snake on the tree in between the branches. Sandra pointed towards it prompting Laura to look, too. The snake looked back at them. They walked near the snake.

"Hello, Ladies!" said the snake.

"What? The snake talks?" exclaimed Laura.

The snake changed its form to a beautiful man. Both the women were quite surprised and amused.

"Here at Paradise, we are all at your service. We can change any shapes, any forms, and will do anything to make you happy because you are the chosen ones of Lehasha," explained the snake man.

Laura and Sandra continued to look at the snake man in amazement. The snake man looked back at them with a seductive look and asked, "Can I be of service?"

This was a bit too much for the ladies who started to giggle. The snake-man plucked an apple from the tree and took a deep bite into it. He extended the apple towards the ladies and prompted, "Wanna taste my apple?"

Sandra was caught off guard and found it difficult to keep her eyes off his well-toned body. Laura giggled and shook her head no. The snake man moved a little closer towards the ladies. It took another bite of the apple and said in a seducing voice, "There is nothing forbidden in this paradise. All these fruits are yours. Just take it if you want it."

The snake man again extended his arm towards Laura and said, "Come on. Taste it now."

Laura smiled and replied, "No, not now." She started to walk away from the snake man and waved at Sandra.

"Come on. Let's go. He's teasing us. Let's run," said Laura.

Sandra rushed towards Laura and they bolted away.

"I'll be here whenever you want to come," said the snake man waving at them. The women ran through the trees laughing. They hadn't felt so care-free in years.

Chapter XX

Lifting the Veil

Rachel had been wandering the streets since morning. She still had the sketch in her hands. While walking, she came across a building that had "Maya's Paradise" written on its entrance. She compared it to the picture in her hand. To her amazement, it was identical. She couldn't believe her luck.

Was her mother trying to send a message to her? What was it that her mother wanted to communicate to her?

Rachel didn't really know what to do next, so she simply stood in the street. With curiosity taking the best of her, she walked towards the door.

A drop of water fell on Sandra's face. She stopped and looked towards the sky. Laura was also looking at the sky. Laura extended her arms into the falling water drops. They enjoyed the droplets splashing on their faces.

Rachel opened the door and peeped in. The wind chime hanging on the door rang in a melodious tune. The place looked like a yoga center.

Laura and Sandra enjoyed the rain and ran through the trees some more. Maya and Tony approached them. Maya stood there smiling. She gestured and a lady appeared with a tray of apples in her hand. Maya beckoned Laura to have an apple.

Rachael walked inside to see a group of people sitting in a circle on the floor. They were engrossed in deep meditation.

Laura and Sandra walk up to Maya. Suddenly, Laura felt a hole open in the floor, and she and Sandra fall into it.

Rachel felt confused. She had never thought any such thing existed in their city. She stood there looking at them and realized that they were trying to open their eyes as if rising from a deep sleep.

Maya opened her eyes and saw Rachel standing in the room. She looked at Tony as if asking how the girl was able to enter.

Tony walked up to the door to check it. He shrugged.

Rachel felt uneasy and walked back towards the door.

"Stop," ordered Maya. She resumed chanting, withdrew her hands from the people sitting around her.

With the human chain broken, others began opening their eyes. The chanting stopped.

The light from the magic ball faded and the smoke slowed down.

Tony walked up to Rachel and enquired, "Wasn't the door locked?"

"No, it was open. I just walked in," answered Rachel with hesitation.

"Well, that's strange. I think I locked it," said Tony.

Rachel looked at Maya and the light ball. She felt an urge to look at the paper in her hand but chose hide her hand behind her back.

Maya looked into Rachel's eyes as if she was trying to read her mind. Rachel evaded eye contact with Maya. She could feel something was not right, and it scared her.

Chapter XXI

Beyond the Known

The group was ready to leave Maya's Paradise. Sandra and Laura walked out together. Tessa followed them closely.

"That was another awesome session," said Tessa.

"True. I really enjoyed it until the interruption," said Sandra.

"It's okay. There's always next week," replied Laura.

The girls waved goodbye to Ouso, who was already in his car nearby. With a wave, he drove out of the parking lot.

"Bye, girls!! See you next week," said Tessa rushing towards the car.

Both of them waved at her and came to stand in front of the building adjoining Maya's Paradise.

"Aren't you excited? Just 3 more weeks until the carnival, and we're going to perform there," said Laura.

"Yes, I am. My first performance as a dancer. Kind of unexpected though," replied Sandra.

After a few moments of silence, Laura said, "I invited Maya as the chief guest to the carnival."

"Did you? What did she say?" asked Sandra, who was a little surprised to hear this.

"She said yes, of course! She's surprised that we're planning a carnival in this town," said Laura.

"Oh, that's nice if she has agreed to come," said Sandra. The worry lines deepened on her face. She was concerned about something.

"You're not nervous, are you?" asked Laura.

"Well, now I am! I keep forgetting the dance steps. What is the step after this?" She demonstrated the movement to Laura." That's the thing I always forget," said Sandra with a smile. She didn't want Laura to realize that she was feeling tense.

"Is that like this?" asked Sandra while showing another step.

"Yeah, almost like that, but more like this," said Laura while showing her how to do the step.

"Ok, let me try," said Sandra.

Sandra repeated the steps until she had them in her memory. A few people passed by and look at them practicing. They are amused. A car coming from the other side of the street caught her attention and she stopped.

"Your hubby is coming," said Sandra.

Laura looked at the car and stopped dancing.

"That's okay. Let me know when you're free so we can practice again," said Laura.

"Next week for sure. I'm kind of busy now," said Sandra smiling back.

"Fine," responded Laura.

The car neared them and stopped. Steve, Johnny, and Amy were all in the car. The children had story books in their hands. Sandra waved to the kids and they waved back.

Both women walked towards the car.

"Hi Steve, how are you?" asked Sandra.

"Great, Sandra. How about you?" Steve replied.

"I'm ok. Keeping busy" replied Sandra

Steve nodded his head.

"I heard you're buying that old church. What are you planning to do there?" questioned Sandra.

It came as a surprise for Steve that Sandra already knew about the church deal when he had taken extra efforts to ensure not to let out the news.

"Oh yeah...Yes. The price was low because the whole place needs renovation, so we took advantage of the deal. I haven't decided what to do there yet. But who told you that?" asked Steve.

"Oh, it's a small town. News travels fast," said Sandra with a smile.

"How are the kids? Are they ok with the new school?" continued Sandra.

"They're ok. Amy has been a little upset lately. Guess she's missing her friends in New York. Johnny is young and seems to have adjusted better. He adjusts rather well to anything," said Laura.

Steve looked at Sandra and smiled. "By the way, how is your tantric guru...Maya? Did you also feel the same out-of-the-world experience that my wife says she had?"

Laura and Sandra exchanged a look amongst themselves.

"Yes...I do, and everybody else does also. Maya is very gifted. Her meditation is really an otherworldly experience. I don't know how to explain it," said Sandra. Her voice was full of adulation for Maya.

"Do you think she has some powers? Some people say she is an evil worshipper and knows black magic. There are rumors that she is a witch." asked Steve.

"I don't know. The people in this town, they talk a lot of crazy stuff. They just want booze and drugs. I don't know if Maya has any powers or not, but I do know that people are scared of her," said Sandra in a concerned voice.

They were silent for a few seconds. Steve looked at Laura.

"Okay, Sandie. We have to go now. The kids are hungry," said Laura grinning at Sandra.

"Bye," said Sandra.

"Bye, Sandra," said Steve caressing Amy's hair.

Sandra waved while Laura got into the car.

"See you kids!" said Sandra and smiled back at the kids.

"Bye, bye! See you soon," said Amy.

"See you!" shouted Johnny and waved at Sandra. She waved back one last time.

Steve drove off. A few minutes later he looked at Laura. Taking her hand in his, he pecked a kiss on it.

Laura smiled back and pressed his hand tightly.

Steve looked at the children in the review mirror and saw that they were busy in their story books.

They reached a point on the road where two people were involved in a fight right in the middle of the driving lanes. "Oh, no not again? So many crimes. Is there no law and order in this town? No police station to complain to?" worried Laura.

"No, they closed down the police station many years back. I heard nobody wanted to work here. They're scared of death," replied Steve.

"By whom?" said Laura, shocked.

"Nobody knows who can be held responsible for this. But from what I heard I am sure doubt it is her' said Steve. He slowed down a little in order to take a closer look at the two men fighting.

Laura didn't understand what Steve was talking about. She gave him a confused look.

"Maya!" said Steve.

"Maya?" repeated Laura as they drove away.

Chapter XXII

The Connecting Strings

Maya was seated right in front of Rachel and looking deep into her eyes.

There was absolute silence in the room, but their minds were loud with questions about the one sitting across from them. Both wanted to know more.

It's really nice that you want to join the group," said Maya.

Rachel chose not to speak and just nodded her head.

"But, may I ask why?"

Rachel knew that she would have to answer some questions when she met with Maya about joining the group, but when the actual question cropped up, she felt confused and at a loss for words.

Rachel shrugged her shoulders and, as an afterthought, said, "Nothing much."

"People come here for different reasons. Some want to fill in their time, some want to relax, while others want to connect to their mystical powers," said Maya.

She did not lift her eyes from Rachel.

"But, some people come here for hidden reasons," continued Maya.

Rachel could feel that she was under Maya's gaze continuously.

Rachel lifted her head and looked at Maya surprised. They made eye contact for the first time.

Rachel quickly looked away. She felt Maya's eyes penetrating deep into her.

"I know you didn't come here to join our group," continued Maya.

"Am I correct?" she pried after being silent for a few minutes.

"Your eyes tell me you are either worried or scared of something," said Maya.

The moment Rachel heard this she again looked at Maya. It was as if Maya had read her mind.

"Either way, I can help you. To help you, I must know you."

It was now on Rachel to decide what she wanted to tell Maya about herself .

They were silent for a few seconds. Rachel looked at Maya and hesitantly asked, "Can you speak to the spirits?"

"Yes, I can. Whom do you want to speak to?" asked Maya.

"My mother passed away a few months back. I just wanted to know if she is alright," said Rachel.

Maya kept quiet and closed her eyes for a minute. She opened her eyes and looked straight into Rachel's eyes. Maya extended her hands for Rachel to hold.

Rachel extended her hands and placed them in Maya's. Maya then closed her eyes and started to chant in whispers.

Rachel couldn't keep her eyes open for long. They closed on their own.

With her eyes closed, it was now only Maya's voice that gave her a sense of place.

Maya's cat got up from the carpet and started to move around in a circular motion. After a few circles it walked towards Rachel and circled her.

Unmindful of the cat circling her, Rachel kept her eyes closed. She could still hear the chants, and Rachel's mind started to play tricks on her. She heard footsteps as if a child was running around. The child seemed to be breathing hard. She saw Grace and herself as a kid climbing up a mountain. They see a police car parked on the edge of the road.

Rachel could see the excitement on her childhood face upon seeing the car. It was her father's duty car.

"Daddy!" shouted little Rachel. She ran towards the car. Grace was close behind.

On reaching the car, little Rachel felt confused. There was no one in the car. She opened the front door and climbed in. Her father was nowhere to be seen.

"Daddy! Daddy, where are you?" shouted little Rachel coming out of the car. She wanted to see her father and every delay was only making her more and more restless. Even as a child, she could sense that all was not well for the three of them.

Grace searched in and around the car. Yes, it was her husband's car, but where was he? Days later, news spread in the town that a police car was parked on the hill top. Since there had been no news about Richard for the last few days, the mother and daughter rushed to see if it was his car. Grace opened the trunk, but found no one there. Suddenly, the otherwise quiet hill-top was filled with Grace and Rachel's voices. While Grace was calling out, "Richard," Rachel was calling out, "Daddy."

With every passing minute, the confusion rose. Grace ran towards the edge of the cliff. She saw Richard's police badge and a piece of cloth stuck on a tree. She did not want to believe what she saw.

Grace started to cry frantically and kept shouting, "Richard, Richard!" She looked at the cliff, which looked ugly and draconian at this moment. Her sound echoed through the valley.

Rachel saw herself walking towards her mother. She heard her mother say, "Oh, my God! That witch killed him!"

Grace cried uncontrollably and said repeatedly, "Richard. Oh God, that witch!"

Rachel saw her little self crying. It was not easy to see her mother distraught and shattered. Grace grabbed Rachel. Both mother and daughter were crying hysterically.

Inside Maya's Paradise, Rachel still had her hands in Maya's.

Tears were flowing down Rachel's cheeks. She could still hear her mother's voice, "Oh, my God. That witch killed him! Richard. Oh, God! That witch!"

Rachel opened her eyes and looked at Maya. For a flash of a second, instead of Maya she saw an old witch who had her face covered with a black shawl. She was startled and frightened. A cat was sitting next to this old witch. The cat looked at Rachel and made a wild sound. Rachel looked at her hands and saw that they were in the hands of a skeleton.

Rachel looked at Maya. Scared and shocked, she pulled her hands off and tried to stand up and run. The cat jumped at her hissing and growling.

This was enough to break Maya's chanting. She opened her eyes and looked at Rachel.

"What happened?" asked Maya.

Rachel looked at Maya again, but this time she did not appear like a witch. Taking a deep breath, she pointed towards the cat and said, "Your cat... it jumped at me."

Maya looked at the cat which had come to stand near Rachel.

"Oh, don't worry. It's just Billie!" said Maya.

"He's very friendly," continued Maya and signaled the cat to come towards her.

The cat ran up to Maya who lifted it in her lap and started to play with it. Rachel looked worried. She was sure she was imagining things.

"Don't worry. He won't harm you. Sit back," said Maya in an authoritative voice.

Rachel obeyed.

"Did you get what you came for?" asked Maya, once again piercing Rachel with her eyes.

"Something sent you here. Something told you to come find me." continued Maya.

Rachel was surprised that Maya knew about the note.

"Yes," said Rachel, and then she went silent.

"If you want me to call your mother's spirit, hold my hands. I can bring her here, and you can talk to her through me. It will take some time, though," stated Maya.

Rachel was confused. Something was telling her to run away from this place, but, yes, she felt tempted to meet her mother's spirit.

'Oh, no. I don't think that would be a good idea now,' said Rachel.

"Spirits and souls, they exist and are everywhere. But humans cannot see them just like you cannot see the air or electricity, even though they are sources of great power. The spirits may be sitting next to you and laughing and crying with you, but you cannot see them," said Maya.

After a brief pause Maya said, "Any time you want to speak to your mother, let me know. I can call her spirit. You can talk to her through me."

"Hmm...' considered Rachel.

"We meet here every week. You are welcome to join us and learn to live in harmony with nature and experience the power and presence of super natural force. If you join us, I can fulfill all of your wishes, desires, and wants. And you will become chosen to serve the powerful Lord," said Maya.

Rachel nodded her head to signal that she understood what Maya was telling her. Maya looked closely into Rachel's face. It was not Rachel's, but Grace's face, that she was seeing.

"It was nice to meet with you, Maya. I look forward to seeing you again," said Rachel in Grace's voice.

Maya was confused. This had never happened with her before. She looked again trying to concentrate on Rachel's face. What she saw now was not Grace but Rachel again.

"I will come for the next session," said Rachel rising from her seat.

"Sure. I look forward to seeing you again," said Maya.

Maya was straining her mind to determine where she had seen the other face. Rachel started to leave.

"Rachel?" Maya called out.

Rachel turned back.

"I saw your mother was in a wheelchair. What happened to her?" asked Maya.

"Oh, she fell into a pit. It happened long ago when I was a child," said Rachel.

"That's ok. Just wondering," said Maya.

Rachel smiled and turned to leave. The cat made a wild sound. As Rachel walked out, she looked at the various snakes in the cages and statues. Maya studied Rachel as she left, concerned about Rachel's intentions.

Chapter XXIII

A Walk through Memories

Sandra had noticed all the attention that Maya was paying to Rachel during the session. While walking towards the hill Rachel's innocent eyes played before her. She hated coming here but there was no escape. Every moonless night she was forced to come here. Today thinking about Rachel made it all the more difficult for her. She knew what the future or rather Maya had in store for Rachel.

On her way up, Sandra noticed a burnt-off tree. She remembered the first time that she had seen the tree. It was green and beautiful with purple flowers strewn on the ground. For a minute, she wondered what had happened to it. She remembers herself being dragged to the mountain top by Ouso and Ben. Their strong grip on her arms was hurting her. She had a cotton sling bag on her shoulders. She gripped the bag, but it offered no help in her situation.

Sandra tried to fight back and free herself from their grip. All her fighting and jostling was making it difficult for Ouso and Ben to drag her. Ouso had closed her mouth tightly and slapped her on the face resulting in tears to roll down her cheeks.

Once they reached the mountain top, Sandra saw three wooden crosses with corpses hanging on them. Ouso pushed Sandra to the ground. She landed close to the third corpse. Sandra fainted at the sight of the three corpses. Near each of the cross on the ground, circles with black ink were marked. There were skeleton heads placed in these circles. Dried blood from the corpses had made streams and left its mark on the ground. The blood was feeding the fire.

Ouso traced a circle with the index finger of his right hand near the fourth cross. Ouso took out a skeleton head from a cotton bag and placed the head in the circle. The moment he did this, the fire flared as if trying to reach the sky.

Sandra lay there unconscious until the next morning.

Sandra awoke to the sound of Maya's chanting. She sees Maya chanting. Ouso and Ben are standing near her. Sandra found herself naked and chained to a wooden cross in the ground. She cried helplessly pulling on the chains around her wrist. The crow was watching them from the tree top.

Sandra looks at Maya and asks her, "Who are you? Please don't harm me."

"Let me go. Please," Sandra had pleaded.

From far away Tony was running to the top of the mountain. He had been severely beaten up. Blood was dripping from his face and he appeared to be in pain.

Maya had raised her right hand and said a chant. A sword had appeared in her right hand.

"Lehasha, my master, please accept the soul of this unblemished girl as my sacrificial offering to you," Maya prayed as she walked up to Sandra.

"Please, please, don't kill me," pleaded Sandra.

Maya circled Sandra. Suddenly, Tony appeared at the scene and ran towards Maya and Sandra. "Stop. Don't harm her."

Tony's sudden appearance had disturbed Maya. She frowned and looked at Ouso and Ben. Her voice roared, "Who is that?"

"That's her brother. He fought with us, and we hit him hard. I thought he was dead," replied Ouso.

Sandra had looked at Tony and started crying. Amidst her cries she said, "Brother. Save me, Brother."

Tony ran up to Sandra. Holding his sister he shouted, "Leave her alone."

Ouso and Ben pounced on him and started beating him recklessly. Tony, though wounded, tried to fight them back. His strength and well-built body caught Maya's attention.

"Please, please, don't harm my brother. Please let us go," begged Sandra.

Tony was able to overpower Ouso and Ben. Every time he looked at Sandra, he seemed to get more and more strength to free his sister.

Tony got hold of a stick and used it to beat Ouso and Ben. He aimed the stick at Maya. This angered her. She outstretched her right hand in the direction of Tony and said a chant. Tony immediately froze in his place. Seeing all of this, Sandra began to pull at the chains with all her strength. Her only hope of escape was her brother who had become a veritable statue. "What did you do to my brother?" shouted Sandra.

Maya picked up the sword and walked towards Tony. She wanted to kill him.

"Please, don't kill my brother. Please, kill me and let him go. Please," continued Sandra.

Maya was standing near Tony. She found it difficult to keep her eyes off Tony's chest. She could hear Sandra plead in the background.

"My brother spent his whole life raising me. Please, take my life instead of his. At least I can die knowing I did something in return for all the great things my brother did for me. Please, don't kill him," cried Sandra. Maya raised the sword in the air. Ouso and Ben stood up in anticipation of what was about to happen.

"But, if you spare our lives, we can be your servants. We have nobody else in this world. I promise we will be truthful to you until our death, and we will serve you,' said Sandra. She was ready to do anything to save her brother from the clutches of these evil worshippers.

Maya seemed confused. She was attracted to Tony, but was unsure how to respond to the offer. Maya kept the tip of her sword on Tony's chest and asked, "Do you promise what she says?"

Tony nodded his head in the affirmative.

Maya looked at Ouso and signaled him to open Sandra's chains. She outstretched her right hand in the direction of Tony and said a chant which freed Tony from the effect of the statue spell.

Sandra ran up to Tony and they hugged fiercely.

Snapping out of her thoughts, Sandra continued to walk until she reached the top of the mountain. She saw eight corpses hanging on wooden crosses. Near each of the cross on the ground, circles with black ink were marked. There were skeleton heads placed in these circles. Her eyes traced the dried blood from the streams, which were running to a campfire where an angry fire flared.

Sandra looked at the ninth cross without a corpse. She walked up to the ninth cross. She knelt down and drew a circle with her fingers. As soon as the circle is drawn it turns black. She took the skeleton head from her bag and placed it in the ninth circle.

Sandra looked at the skeleton heads. Her eyes stopped on the fourth head. Instead of the dead girl, she imagined herself hanging from the wooden cross. Sandra makes a sigh of relief. She stands up and leaves.

Chapter XXIV

The Unsaid Words

It had been a busy day for Laura and Steve. Little Johnny had gotten hurt in school while playing.

Finally back home, Laura went to her bedroom after settling the kids in bed. Steve was sitting on the bed reading the bible. She stood in front of the dresser combing her hair. She looked at Steve again through the mirror.

Laura walked up to the bed and settled herself. She pulled the cover over her body and took Steve's left hand in hers.

Steve turned towards her. Laura seemed to be lost in some deep thoughts.

"You ok?" asked Steve.

"Oh, nothing" replied Laura.

"Sure? Does something worry you?" asked Steve again wanting to be sure.

Laura had a confused look on her face. She continued playing with Steve's hand and asked, "Do you think Maya is the darkness that covered this town?"

"I don't know. I found details of some of the people who left this town and called them. Many of them said she is an evil-worshiper. They say that it was after her coming to the town that all the deaths and bad things started to happen. They believe she's a Witch," reported Steve.

Laura's eyes met Steve's. Steve knew that Laura was worried. He could feel that she was not comfortable at Maya's.

"What is your experience at her place? Do you think what they said may be true?" asked Steve.

"I don't know, but there is something suspicious about her. She has some powers, good or bad. I still don't know. Her place is very scary with snakes and statues. It is like a palace of evil gods," said Laura.

Their eyes met again.

"You know I'm not a false believer. But trust me, once she starts her chanting, I don't know if it's the smoke or the atmosphere... I think... I feel like I'm in a dream like some type of a paradise," said Laura.

"Paradise?" asked Steve.

"Yes. Maya made all her disciples believe there is an evil god called Lehasha, and that she will join with him on a dark moon day. Once she gets the power, her disciples will be privileged, and they will live with her in paradise. All those people there truly believe that the evil god will come, and they will be chosen to serve him," continued Laura.

Steve looked at her worried.

"I knew she was a bad omen. I had a very bad feeling from the first time I met her. That statue of ours that broke when she visited was trying to tell me something... Probably to prevent Maya from destructing this town. I wanted to confirm my intuition was correct," said Steve taking her both hands in his.

Laura placed her head on Steve's shoulder. Caressing her hair Steve said, "That is why I requested you to join her and see what is happening there at her place."

Laura raised her eyes to look at Steve. "But if she is evil, and there is some dark force as she says, and the people you contacted have told you, is it safe for me to be there?" she asked.

"I'm a little nervous about this," she added after a pause.

Steve held her hand to his heart and said, "Babe, you know we came to this town for a purpose. The people in this town are on a path of destruction. I don't know who killed my uncle, but I do know that my uncle may have sacrificed his life to save this town. We need to know who the evil forces are and how powerful they are. That is the only way we can destroy them."

They both looked at each other for a moment.

"Please, hold on until the carnival. Please, try to find out what she is planning on the dark moon. We need to do something before the dark moon in order to prevent her from getting powers. If she gets more powers, it will be very difficult to defeat her. This city will be doomed forever. I want you to be there so I can know what she is planning. Be very friendly and close to that girl Sandra. She may know a lot of secrets about Maya. Try to find something from her, and also see if she will join us to protect this town," continued Steve.

Steve was quiet for a few minutes. He seemed to be deep in thought planning something.

"I have a plan. I will call our prayer group in New York tomorrow to discuss it. I know it's risky, but we have to do it,

Baby. We have to protect this town. As true Christians, that is our duty," he said in a decisively.

Laura looked at Steve. Even though it was very comforting to speak to Steve, she was still worried. She wanted to hear Steve tell her not to go back to Maya's. She wanted to tell Steve to leave the town.

The clock struck midnight. Steve pointed at the clock and said, "Come on sweetheart. Go to sleep. Don't think much about Maya at this hour."

Laura placed her head on the pillow, and Steve caressed her hair. Within minutes, she was sleeping soundly. Steve slid out of the bed quietly and went to the living room. He was restless.

Chapter XXV

Offering

Once again, the life of a young girl was doomed. Anita was being dragged to the mountain top by Ouso and Ben. She was crying, pleading the men to let her go.

"What are you doing? Leave me," cried Anita.

She tried to push Ben with her legs, but he was too strong for her. All the pushing and jostling made Ben irritable. He stood over her, and beat the girl harshly. Blood started dripping from her mouth, and she cried in pain. Upon reaching the mountain top, she saw the corpses, streams of blood, and skeleton heads. She shrieked in fear, and her whole body quaked with shivers. She had no idea where she was or why these people brought her here. She knew she had to escape from here. Clearly, eight other people had not.

"Oh, my God!...my God! Don't kill me, please!" She tried once again to run away, but Ouso was quick enough to catch her. He threw her towards Ben, who dragged her towards the cuffs and the chains. While Ben held on to her, Ouso fastened the chains.

Once they were finished, they started to walk away. Not wanting to be left there to die, Anita shouted, "Oh, God! Don't leave me. Come back. Take me with you. I will give everything I have. Please don't leave me here."

Without even looking at her, they continued to walk away.

Anita screamed for help long after the men had gone, but there was only her and it was only the corpses left on the mountain top.

Chapter XXVI

The Carnival Comes to Town

Rachel stood at the door of her house searching in her bag for her keys. She was always reluctant to come home. She hated coming back to an empty house, yet that's where she found herself once again

She stepped into the living room and saw her mother's empty wheel chair. She had often thought of donating the wheel chair to someone needy, but never followed through with the idea because it reminded her of her mother. She would often sit on the floor in front of the chair and place her head on its seat just as she would place her head in her mother's lap.

She walked up to her mother's picture on the wall and stood in front of it. Taking a deep breath, she moved to the calendar hanging on the wall. After marking "Meeting with Maya" on the day's date, she walked over to the wheel chair.

"Mother, can you hear me? Why did you draw this picture?" Rachel gripped the drawing while looking at wheelchair as if her mother was sitting in it.

"What does this picture mean? What do you want me to do at that place?" she continued.

Her mind was full of questions, and she wanted answers. She was sure that it was her mother who had drawn the picture, but Rachel was unable to figure out why.

"I'm confused. Do you want me to go there again?"

She was silent for a minute.

She walked back to the calendar.

"Mom, I'm really, really scared to go there. I think she's a witch, a cruel witch, and the whole place is creepy," said Rachel.

The empty wheelchair made her feel really lonely.

Suddenly breaking into her deep thought was a lot of noise coming from the street. An announcement was being made on a loudspeaker.

She opened the main door to see what was going on and saw a horse cart moving down the street. There were two people on the cart. While one was driving it, the other was making an announcement.

"Carnival at Bridgeport! The event you've been waiting for. Circus performers, jokers, dancers, children's rides, and free food," a voice was heard over the mike.

A group of people who were sitting across the street started walking towards the cart. It had been years since anything this exciting had happened in the town. Since Father Mario's death, everything had been boring and dark.

"Lots of free food, lots of fun and colorful dances. Come to the Carnival. The event that Bridgeport was waiting for. Come, and attend," continued the announcements.

The other man distributed some pamphlets to the people standing around.

Chapter XXVII

Endowment

The crow flew over the entrance of the city like a guard for Maya. It watched all of the people entering and exiting the city. After some wide circles around the township, it perched itself on the welcome sign and looked around. Suddenly, it heard Maya's voice. She was chanting, calling to him. It was time for the crow to go to his master. It took off straight towards the mountain top.

Maya and Tony were present atop the mountain when the crow arrived. While Maya chanted fervently, Tony watched. Amongst the corpses lay helpless Anita; she was chained to the ninth set of cuffs and bleeding badly from her throat. The crow perched on the tree.

Tony looked at the chained bodies and then at Anita. Maya signaled to him, and he approached her once more to stab her in the throat. Anita let out a faint cry. She felt the pain, but was too weak even to let out a shriek. She had lost a lot of blood. The crow watched all of this keenly.

Tony walked back to Maya, who was still chanting. Her voice became louder echoing through the entire area.

Quickly, a whirl wind surrounded them both. A circle of light appeared around Maya, and Tony closed his eyes.

The cloud of light subdued and a voice spoke. An old woman appeared in front of Maya with a jar of blood in her hands.

"I am Louhan, the servant of the Lord, Lehasha. I have been sent to give you this." Wrinkled hands offered the jar to Maya.

"This is the blood of the Lord. It should be passed to your womb through a human as instructed in the book," continued Louhan.

Tony couldn't see anything except a circle of light around Maya.

"Remember, the human must be converted and he must accept Lehasha as the master and Lord. It is all explained in the book."

"I will carry out his wishes properly," replied Maya as she touched the jar to her forehead.

The circle of light disappeared. The old lady was gone.

Tony walked towards Maya. He had his eyes fixed on the jar of blood.

The crow was a mute witness to all the plans carried out on the mountain top.

Chapter XXVIII

Tribulations

The carnival was scheduled and all of the arrangements finalized. The park in the center of town flashed with decorations and the lights of rides and attractions. Canopies of different colors, streamers, and balloons swayed in the breeze. The residents were happy, young and old. Everyone waited excitedly for the event that begins the next day.

Sandra walked into the carnival area. On seeing her walk into the park, Laura rushed towards her. They hugged and wandered off to chat about the upcoming events. The lights were getting set up by a group of men who started near the gate. Steve, Michael along with Jordy and Angelo worked to get the string of lights secured. All four had been good friends for quite some years now and had supported each other through thick and thin.

As Sandra walked past the group, Steve quietly pointed her out to the others. "That's Sandra, one of Maya's disciples. She and a few others are on the program, so we have a good reason to invite Maya." They all stole a look at her.

"That was a good idea, but be careful," said Michael.

"Do you think she'll get suspicious of strangers here and notify Maya?"' asked Jordy.

"No, don't worry. We invited her for rehearsal and told her that people from our dance troop will be here today," said Steve.

"That's ok. She may think we're from that dance troupe," said Michael.

Laura and Sandra were joined by Monica and Srini, who were already in their costumes for dance practice.

Laura introduced Srini and Monica to Sandra while Steve and the others continued talking in hushed tones.

"The next dark moon day Maya will join with Lehasha and get enormous powers. We don't know if it's true or if she is just trying to make others believe that, but if it is true, she will become even more dangerous. That's why I called all of you for assistance," said Steve.

"So, what's our plan?" asked Michael.

Steve bent closer towards them secretively. The others listened.

"As soon as Maya reaches the carnival, we need to get inside her center and see what we can find about her plans. I heard she has a crystal ball and that she recites from some old books. We need to find what gives her the power and destroy it. We need to kill all the snakes and break all the statues. Everything she uses for evil worship should be destroyed. We should bring that place down completely. In the future, Maya shouldn't be able to have any disciples or perform any black magic. I think she'll lose the power if she has no place to worship," said Steve.

"We should also sprinkle holy water and hang crosses and rosaries on the walls," suggested Michael.

"Yes that will surely destroy her evil powers," said Jordy in approval.

"Well, let's give it a try. But, if she still continues her evil magic, we need to plan something more vigorous," said Steve.

"I think we should tie her up and burn that witch alive. That's how the church killed the witches in the past," ranted Angelo.

"I've done some research in the manuscripts about Witches. Before we do something so drastic, let's see if she can change. We should pray for her conversion," said Steve.

They group glanced over at Sandra and Laura practicing the dances. Steve mentions, "I tried to make the show very colorful to attract Maya's taste, and there is nothing religious in the program, so she won't be suspicious. Maya should keep watching it until the end. Before she gets back to the center we should finish destroying that place, okay?" continued Steve looking keenly at the others for approval and support.

"Okay," they all said, and Steve nodded in approval.

"I am worried that the witch can read minds, so I haven't told Laura about our plans. Don't discuss anything in front of her or Sandra,' ordered Steve.

"So Laura doesn't know why we have come?" asked Michael.

"No, she doesn't. She goes to the center to learn her secrets and to spy on what is she is doing. If that witch knows black magic, I'm worried she'll be able to read minds. So, if Laura knows about our plans, the witch may find out," said Steve.

"Okay, good call," said Jordy and gave thumbs up sign to Steve.

Michael went quiet. He was worried for Laura. He recognized the danger Laura and the rest of them were in.

Laura and Sandra continued dancing.

Steve signaled the others in the group to hold hands. They said a prayer, "Empower us, Oh God, to destroy the evil in this town. We ask for your help and guidance. Please, prevent this town from suffering Maya's evil and destruction. We want the people here to believe in God and turn away from evil forces. We want to reopen the church doors. We want the church to be active again. Please help us, Oh Lord. In Jesus' name I pray. Amen."

Steve released the hands of the men at his sides and opened his eyes. He was ready to take down the evil.

Chapter XXIX

The Forbidden Fruit

Maya's Paradise was empty when Rachel opened the door to enter. She looked around and found no one. As she entered the room, the white snake hissed at her. Rachel walked across the room and sat in a corner. She looked around. She was scared. Her hands automatically reached to the cross in her neck.

"I don't know why Mom wanted me to come here. That witch scares me. Oh God, please save me," murmured Rachel to herself.

Rachel had been in the room only for a few minutes when some members started to walk in.

A middle aged woman greeted Rachel.

"Hi," replied Rachel in a clipped manner. She wanted to blend in and make friends, but she was so scared that Rachel mostly wanted to avoid the others.

The group prepared for their meditation, and Laura walked up to Rachel and asked her to join them.

"All these girls do they even know what they are getting into? Do they know that lady is a witch? A witch that can control them and destroy their lives?" thought Rachel.

Maya and Tony walked into the room from the other side. Maya greeted the members and raised her hand blessing the group. She walked to her seat and got ready for chanting.

Tony burned the incense and circulated throughout the room. He lit the candles and the lamps placed around the room.

Maya looked at Rachel. She stared at her as if trying to read her mind. Tony finished lighting the candles, and he sat next to Maya.

Rachel could feel Maya's eyes on her. She tried to pay attention to her, but couldn't look into her eyes for long. She felt better after she closed her eyes. Eye contact with Maya made her so uneasy.

Maya opened a book and started chanting. The group repeated after Maya.

Rachel heard a voice ringing in her ears. She paid attention and realized that her mother was trying to say something to her, "Rachel, my child, do not pay attention to her voice. Do not look at her. Do not repeat the words. Keep your eyes shut, and keep praying that you do not fall into her spell."

Rachel, feeling panicked, was about to open her eyes in order to see from where the voice was coming, but felt a soft touch on her eyelids as if her mother wanted her to keep them closed. She took a deep breath and held on to the cross. Rachel felt better and safer knowing her mother's presence was around her.

"Let the power of the universe fill this room. Let the power of light and darkness fills this room. Let the power that can control the humans fill this room," chanted Maya, and the group repeated behind her.

The lights in the room began to blink. A wind started to blow in the room. It seemed to be moving in circles. Maya continued to chant in a loud voice.

Rachel opened her eyes and looked around. She felt all of the people sitting around her were in a spell. She looked closely at

Maya and heard the sound of chanting rise. Maya's face looked wild in a spell. Rachel again touched the cross around her neck. Every time she got back to the cross, she felt reassured.

On the other side, Maya felt that she was standing at the door step of paradise. She could see green and blossoming apple trees and a beautiful waterfall. She started strolling in the garden. The group-members moved around happily in the garden. While one girl chased butterflies, Monica stood with the snake man and another person. They were licking each other and sharing an apple. Another girl flew around in the garden trying to chase bubbles. Walking toward the tree where Rachel sat in its shade in meditation, she watched for a while.

Back in the center, Rachel could hear her mother's voice warning, "Do not look at Maya or pay attention to her. She is trying to read your thoughts to find your weakness so she can control you. She will tempt you with hopes of a dream paradise and a great life with her."

Maya, in the garden of paradise, shook her head as if dismissing Rachel and walked towards Tessa, who sat near the river. Maya looked at Tessa and realized that she was thinking about Rao and how he had caught hold of her and thrown her on the floor. This time Tessa did not think about all the pain that Rao had given her, but about being caressed by him. She, in turn, kissed him and touched him within her fantasy. Maya saw Tessa giving into Rao's suggestions of physical pleasures and undress in Tessa's thoughts.

Tessa's thoughts came as a surprise for Maya. She failed to understand the way the lesser mortals thought. Maya grinned evilly and moved on.

An apple fell into Rachel's lap from the tree under which she sat. She lifted her hand to grab it, but, once again, she heard her mother's voice telling her to throw away the fruit and abstain from eating it.

Rachel obeyed her mother's voice and threw away the apple. "That is the 'Forbidden Fruit.' It is the fruit of death. Maya created that fruit to deceive the people here. Those who eat will be bound by her spells and will be connected to Maya in spirit," continued her mother's voice.

Maya was continuously observing Rachel. Even when she moved away from her, she continued to watch from the corner of her eyes. She signaled a server to take a tray of apples to Rachel, who picked an apple to ease Maya's suspicions. Rachel wanted to walk out of Maya's range of sight.

Inside the room, a purple light beamed on Rachel.

"Once the fruit is eaten, Maya will be able to enter their bodies and control them anytime she wants. She will make them her slaves forever and use them to seduce, kill, and steal. There is no paradise, only a life of suffering and death for those who join her. Continue praying for strength to resist Maya's spell. Whatever she tries, do not touch or eat that 'fruit of death," said Grace to Rachel.

In the garden of paradise, Maya walked towards Sandra and Laura, who sat together. They seemed to be having a good time, sharing jokes and laughing. Maya smiled at them and said, "You girls are like two love birds enjoying the company of each other. It's fun to watch you."

This made both of them laugh. Sandra moved a little closer to Laura.

"Isn't she cute?" said Sandra looking at Maya.

"Of course she is. Both of you are cute," replied Maya.

Maya plucked an apple from the tree and extended it to Laura. "Have you tasted this? It's good," she said.

Laura shook her head no.

"You should taste it," said Maya handing the fruit to Sandra.

Maya picked up another apple and offered it to Laura.

Laura extended her hand to take the apple, but stopped midway and looked around. She looked at Sandra and then Maya and asked, "Who is that?"

Maya and Sandra both looked at her in confusion. There was no one else around.

"I heard a voice tell me not to eat the fruit of the tree. A girl's voice, I think," said Laura.

Maya looked at Rachel and noticed that she was still in meditation.

"What? Who said that? They just don't want you to have a good time. This is the fruit of paradise," said Maya with irritation.

"And it tastes good," added Sandra.

Maya pointed towards the other girls who seemed to be having a good time. While one of the girls ran after butterflies, Monica was busy kissing guys one after another, and Tessa sat smiling near the river.

"Look at them. They ate the fruit, and they are having a good time," encouraged Maya.

"Let me try," said Sandra. She took a bite of the apple. The expression on her face changed. She relished the apple.

"Oh, so sweet," said Sandra licking the juice that dripped from the apple.

"I love it. So tasty," said Sandra once again taking another bite from it.

"I know. I told you," said Maya with a smile.

Maya offered another apple to Laura and said, "Have it. You'll enjoy it!"

Laura took the apple from Maya, bit into it, and gave it to Sandra. They took turns biting the apple.

Maya looked at Rachel, who was still chanting. Maya glanced at an apple on the tree, and it fell down near Rachel.

Rachel opened her eyes on hearing the thud. She looked around and saw the apple lying near her. When she picked up the apple, she heard her mother's voice still playing in her mind. She understood everything that was happening. Maya was adopting all sorts of tactics to disturb Rachel in her meditation. She wanted her to eat the apple at any cost.

Rachel again heard Grace's voice saying, "Rachel, Rachel, come back, my child. Do not fall into Maya's spell. Do not pay attention to them. Come back, Rachel."

Rachel kept the apple on the ground and resumed her meditation, cross in hand.

Near the river, Tessa held Rao very tightly while Ouso tried to pull her away. Tessa's grip on Rao was very strong. Tony gave an iron rod to Maya, who used it to drive away Rao.

Rao felt a sharp pain in his back when Maya whacked him with the rod. He broke free from Tessa's grip and started to run away. Maya followed him. Suddenly, a flash of lightning appeared and struck him. Tessa started to cry.

Maya and Tony continued watching Rachel. The more time she spent in meditation, the more angered Maya felt.

"I'm not able to read her thoughts. She doesn't even open her eyes. Someone may be guiding her not to eat or touch the fruit. Let's find out who she is and what she wants," thought Maya. She looked at tony.

"Poor girl. She doesn't know who she's playing with," whispered Tony.

Back in the room, the sound of chanting stopped. The light faded, and the wind stopped blowing. Suddenly, everything in the room returned to normal.

Maya opened her eyes and looked around. She was restless even after meditation, for Rachel had not allowed her to penetrate her thoughts. She saw that Rachel was still in meditation. Tony opened his eyes and also looked at Rachel. Slowly, all the other members in the group opened their eyes.

Rachel could feel Maya's and Tony's gazes on her. She wasn't sure what she should do. Knowing that she could not keep her eyes closed forever, she opened her eyes and stood up. She held to her cross and looked straight at Maya. Maya could feel Rachel's eyes piercing her.

All members, including Rachel, got ready to leave. While everyone hugged, Rachel was aloof. Laura and Sandra walked past the white snake in order to leave the room. The snake hissed. Monica follows them. The snake hisses again as she passes it. Monica looked at the snake and felt as if it was telling her, "Come back soon. I'll be here." She smiled back at it.

Next, Rachel walked past the snake. She looked at the snake before shifting her glance to an apple suspended from the ceiling. She wondered whether she was imagining the apple or if the others could simply see it, too.

Maya's eyes followed Rachel out of the room. She had no idea what was preventing Rachel from letting her defense down.

"My sacrificial lamb," uttered Maya with clenched teeth.

Chapter XXX

Resurgence

Rachel was walking back home feeling good about the continuous presence of her mother. Though Maya and Tony had initially made her feel scared and vulnerable, she now felt strong enough to face them. She thought about Steve and wanted to share her experiences with him. She knew he could guide her about her new knowledge.

Rachel noticed that a strange-looking man was sitting at the foot of an old tree beside the street. As she reached the tree, this man tried to speak to her in an odd language.

It was Jerome.

"Ahta...Ahta...Aloshata," he said.

"I'm sorry. What was that you said? I didn't hear it."

Jerome again spoke in his peculiar language and looked around.

Rachel stared at him. "What a weird day! First Maya and Tony, and now this man trying to talk to me in a funny language."

"Ahta...Ahta...Aloshata,"repeated Jerome.

Rachel was confused, so she began to walk again. She could still hear Jerome's voice from a distance.

Rachel continued to walk through the streets. She felt someone was following her. She looked back and found no one. She took a few more steps and felt the same presence again. This time she did not look back but ran towards her house.

She was breathless by the time she reached her house. She fished for the key in her bag, opened the door, and dashed inside. She bolted the door and checked that all of the curtains on the windows were drawn.

Rachel was completely unaware that Jerome sat on top of a tree opposite her house watching.

Chapter XXXI

Commitments

Maya's Paradise was vacant save for Tony and Maya. Her voice could be heard chanting in the empty hall. The incense burned and reflections of light flickered from the ball. A fire lit in the room, and Tony stood in front of it.

In the light of the fire, Maya read the mantras from an old prayer book. The book had some graphic illustrations in it. She poured some oil in the fire, and it flared higher. Every time the fire rose her voice became louder and the chanting faster. She raised her hands in the air and chanted, "Master, Lehasha, the controller of life and death. This is my disciple who believes in you. He knows you are the beginning and the end. Please convert him from a human to one among us. Please accept him as your servant."

A blue powder appeared in her right hand, and she threw it at Tony. He stood still with the blue powder all over his body.

"Give him the strength and power to capture and kill your enemies. Give him the powers of immortality. Let him be my companion to spread your kingdom to the far ends of the world," continued Maya.

Maya got up from her seat and walked towards Tony. The cat lying on the floor near him moved away. She ordered him to turn and place his hands on the book. She pressed his hands and continued to chant loudly. Her voice rose. Something sharp protruded from the illustration on the page against which Tony's hands were pressed. The sharp edges pierced into Tony's hands and blood dripped. As the blood contacted the book, it gave out a light.

Maya's eyes pierced into Tony's. "Are you willing to make a pledge of truthfulness and sincerity to the master?"

"Yes, I am," replied Tony.

"Are you completely willing to accept Lehasha as your master and surrender your mind, body, and soul? To be completely at his service?" asked Maya.

"Yes, I am," replied Tony again.

"With you as the medium, our Lord Lehasha will be born again in this world. It is your duty to serve him and prepare the path for him. Do you promise to assist his journey?" asked Maya.

"Yes, I promise," replied Tony nodding his head.

"If the promise is ever broken, it will bring painful death and destruction for you and all your loved ones. Do you understand?" asked Maya.

"Yes, I do."

Maya lifted an iron rod from the prayer fire. On the top of the rod was the logo of a snake. She placed the burning rod on Tony's throat. He closed his eyes in pain, but did not pull away from the branding.

"With this symbol of you, my Lord, this human is marked as your servant. Let this symbol be on his body forever. Let it be a source of identity and power for him," continued Maya.

The emblem burned into Tony's skin and became permanent.

Maya closed the book and the light decreased. The whirlwind slowed down, and the candles in the room flickered.

Chapter XXXII

Villains and Heroes

On the day of the carnival, people bustled about the venue with excitement. There were a few viewers near the stage to watch the dance performance. Many people stood in front of the food counter. Johnny and Amy sat along with other audience members eagerly waiting for their mother's performance. The lights went off and Johnny spoke in an excited voice, "Amy it's about to start."

A beam of light was focused on the stage. The curtains opened and the dance troupe posed in their places. The troupe members were wearing bright and colorful costumes, and melodious music filled the stage. Johnny pointed at Laura and Sandra who were dancing on the stage.

Maya and Tony walked into the auditorium. They went straight to the front row. Johnny noticed something unusual in the auditorium and pointed, asking Amy to look at it. Both children looked at the crow perched on a high frame in the auditorium.

Maya and Tony watched the performance completely oblivious of what was happening at the center.

Steve, Michael and Jordy and Angelo another person arrived at Maya's Center. At the entrance, Michael tried to open the lock on the front door.

"Open it fast, Michael. Jordy, keep an eye on the street while I'll go and check if we can enter through a window or another door," directed Steve as he stuck around the side of the building.

Steve had only reached the back side when he heard a whistle. Michael had succeeded in opening the door, and all four of them entered.

Even though Steve had tried to get information from Laura about what to expect in the hall, they were surprised to see the snakes in cages, statues spread all over the room, and a fire place in the center.

While one of them started sprinkling holy water around the room, another put holy incense all over. Steve and Michael took out markers from their pockets and made the sign of the cross all over the walls.

All four of them held hands and said a prayer. The moment they did, the snakes started hissing and making terrible sounds. The cat moved in circles in the middle of the room.

The snakes managed to slide out of the cages and crawl towards the infiltrators. The snakes were wild and attacked them. Michael and Jordy caught hold of sticks and started to hit back.

Back in the auditorium, Maya felt disturbed. She could hear the sounds of the snakes. She looked at Tony who was busy enjoying the performance.

Steve explored the room a little more. He was looking for something specific. He saw the crystal globe and lifted it. He said a quick prayer and threw it on the ground shattering it. In place of the globe, he positioned a cross.

Maya again heard the hissing of her snakes. She got up and started to walk out of the ground. Tony followed her. Laura and Sandra saw them leaving the hall while they continued to dance.

Within seconds, their performance ended with a big applause from the viewers.

In Maya's center, Steve was able to kill the white snake. The black snake forced his fangs into Jordy's skin. The moment blood oozed from Jordy's skin, the snake began to grow in size. It grew to amazing proportions. They couldn't do anything except run from the room.

Maya and Tony reached the Paradise. The moment they walked through the gate it was clear to them that all was not well. The front door remained open from the intruders' entries, and Maya could sense the presence of those wishing to damage her.

The moment they stepped in, they realized that the house had been vandalized. Maya was livid at the violation. Her white snake was dead and the black snake moved about freely. The black snake moved towards Maya and swirled itself around her feet. Tony lifted it and placed it back in the cage.

Maya looked around. She knew it was Steve's handiwork.

Chapter XXXIII

Prelude to Change

Rachel wandered through the trees. She heard some strange sounds and looked back to find nothing. She felt scared and started walking quickly. Just like last time, she heard the noises and began to run.

Suddenly, someone stepped in front of her. It was Jerome again. He smiled at her, showing his dirty teeth. Rachel was too scared to even move. Recognizing her fear, his smile decreased to a grin and later to a devil's laughter.

Rachel had no idea what to do. She started running in the opposite direction. She could hear Jerome's laughter even at a distance. Rachel reached home. Without stopping, she barged through the gate and opened the lock with trembling hands. She bolted the house from inside. After her breathing slowed and she felt a little safer, she peeped through the curtains. This time she saw Jerome going up the tree across the street.

She was scared to death. She had no idea who this man was or why he followed. She stood behind closed doors wondering, "Oh God. What is that? Why is he after me?"

She gathered some courage and again peeped through the window. Suddenly a thought struck her," Did Maya send him?"

While Jerome guarded the house from the tree across the street, she sat near the window. As evening came, she felt all the more scared. She switched on the lights in every room. She lit a candle in front of Mother Mary's statue on the shelf and read a verse from the Bible. While reading the verse, she thought of her mother. She remembered an evening when her mother sat near the window reading a red book and when she walked in, her mother asked her to open the window.

"Rachel, can you open that window? I can't write with this light," Grace had said to Rachel.

"Mom, what are you writing?" asked Rachel.

"Nothing honey, just some thoughts," said Grace

Rachel extended her hands for the book.

"Let me see, Mom," said Rachel.

Grace closed the book and looked at Rachel's face.

"No, no, Honey. I just started," said Grace.

Rachel remembered looking at her mother in disappointment.

"Baby, I will show you later when I finish writing it, okay?" Grace had said to console her daughter.

She very well remembered how she longed to see what was in the book. Instead of getting a glimpse at the writing, her mother had asked her to get a glass of water for her. Rachel stood in front of the window thinking about the book. She wondered where it was now and what her mother had been writing in it. She turned towards the wheel chair and stared at it for some time.

Suddenly, as if overpowered by her thoughts, she began searching for the book in the house. She checked all of the drawers, shelves, and cabinets for the book.

She didn't find the red book, but kept searching.

Chapter XXXIV

The Revenge

Steve was travelling. He had gone for a night service in the nearby town and was not expected before the next morning. Steve and Laura's house was on the outskirts of the city, and they had no neighbors close by. A whirlwind passed around the house and entered through an open window.

Laura was inside the house. She had settled the children and was sitting on the bed reading a book. She heard a voice chanting, and she tried to pay attention to it. She placed the book on her chest and started daydreaming. She was surprised to see Maya standing in the corner of the room, but rather than getting angry, she smiled at her.

Suddenly, Maya shifted into a wave of light and entered Laura.

Laura's entire body shivered. She made some wild sounds. Hearing the doorbell, Laura walked through the bedroom and the sitting room to open the main door. Sandra stood at the entrance.

Without an exchange of words, Laura allowed Sandra to come in. She closed the door and walked towards the bedroom with Sandra following her closely.

Standing at the bedroom door, Laura extended her arm to touch Sandra's face. Her eyes moved from Sandra's eyes to her lips to her breasts. She moved closer to Sandra and placed her lips on hers. Sandra responded by closing her eyes. Laura kissed her all over the face and neck passionately.

Laura bit at Sandra's throat, and she, in return, let out a giggle. She pushed Sandra's hair away from her neck and kissed her throat. She caressed Sandra behind the ears and allowed her hands to travel all over her back. On reaching Sandra's rear, Laura gripped tightly and pulled Sandra closer to herself.

Sandra shivered in excitement and moaned. She was feeling high. By this time, Laura's hands were tracing her breasts. She searched out her nipples.

Laura bent down and kissed Sandra's breasts. She started pulling off Laura's top. Once it was off, she moved her hand into her bra and caressed her breasts. The soft breasts and the hard nipples aroused Laura severely. She squeezed at Sandra's breasts. Sandra let out a short cry of pain, but it was clear that she was enjoying it. Laura had slipped off the straps of Sandra's bra and unhooked it.

Sandra moved behind Laura and took the nightgown off of her. Laura wore nothing but red underwear. Sandra came in front, bent down to her knees, and put her face on Laura's stomach. She bit it softly and allowed her hands to travel further down.

Laura moaned. She took Sandra's hand in hers and took her to the bed. At 12:30 at night, the girls were wide awake and hungry for more, probing and groping at each other.

Sandra pushed Laura a little and she fell on the bed. Sandra got on top of her and placed her face on Laura's chest. She moved her hands all over Laura's body. She moved further down and started pulling at Laura's panties with her teeth.

Laura let out a cry in pleasure. She was desperate for more. Another hour passed and the girls still continued with their adventure. They sat on the bed with their legs crossed over each other. Laura took Sandra's face in her hands and kissed and bit her lips passionately.

Sandra, in turn, took Laura's fingers and licked them one by one. She then took her hands in between her legs. Laura began to rub across Sandra's legs.

Their excited sounds could be heard all over the room. They kissed and bit each other. They groped and sucked each other's breasts. They caressed and probed each other's depths in ecstasy.

It was 4:00 in the morning when the two girls went off to sleep, tired and exhausted.

A little later, Steve came back home and entered the bedroom. He was shocked to see Laura and Sandra lying naked in bed, but it was not difficult for him to imagine what had happened last night. "Laura," he shouted.

Laura opened her eyes and looked at him. She started laughing hysterically and Sandra accompanied her.

Suddenly, Steve could hear some voices in the background. He looked around and saw no one except Sandra and Laura. It was Laura speaking to him but it was not her voice.

"Steve, many years ago there was a pastor in this town, and if I remember correctly, he was your uncle. In a room like this, I offered him all the riches and pleasures of the world to join with me and become my disciple. He refused. So, I killed him," said Maya's voice.

Laura looked wild at this moment.

"I killed him and hanged him on that bell that night," said Laura in Maya's voice.

Everything was crystal clear for Steve. His uncle had been murdered by Maya, and at this moment, it was not Laura who was doing all this. Laura was possessed.

There was nothing that Steve could do. He was in shock.

"I know you came here to know find out what happened to your uncle and to reopen that church to spread your religion. I waited to see how far you would go. But..." said Laura in Maya's voice.

Suddenly, Maya moved out of Laura's body and stood right in front of Steve.

Steve stared at Maya.

"You had the gall to enter my place of worship and destroy my valuables," roared Maya moving closer to him.

Steve was scared and shaking.

"No one ever disrespects me," said Maya in a firm voice. She pointed towards Laura.

"Look at your wife. Do you see any love for you in her eyes?" she continued.

Steve turned his head to take a look at Laura. She looked under a spell. He felt bad, because it was his fault that Laura was like that. He thought of all the pain and anguish he had caused to her in order to accomplish his mission.

"She is my slave for the rest of her life. I can enter her body any time I want to and do whatever I want to. You came here to spread religion. However, from today, your wife will spread evil in this town. Each night she will wander the streets looking for prey to kill," announced Maya laughing.

"You set up a carnival to divert my attention. Very nice! That is why I brought her dance partner here. I wanted to show you what your wife really wants," said Maya. She raised her arm, and a sword appeared in her hands. While Laura and Sandra stood motionless, still under a spell, Steve fell on his knees holding the cross around his neck. He knew what destiny had in store for him. He started saying a prayer that the Lord bless his children and take care of them.

"You thought by destroying my place of worship you could destroy my powers. You fool. I am a witch. I can travel in and out of humans' bodies. My mantras are in my lips, in my tongue, in my hands, in my body," said Maya in a cold voice.

She raised the sword and placed it on Steve's throat. "Just like your uncle, you never learn your lesson. So, there is no point in having you here."

Steve closed his eyes and continued to pray. He knew he could not fight it. For his every attempt to fight her, it was Laura, Amy, and Johnny who would have to pay the price.

"No one, no one ever disrespects me," she said just before she stabbed Steve in the chest again and again.

Within a few seconds, Steve lay dead on the floor.

Laura looked at the dead body blankly. She was still under the spell. Maya walked out of the house and Sandra followed. After few moments, Laura followed them.

Chapter XXXV

The Quest

Rachel's entire house was scattered with books, photos, and other items she had tossed aside in her search for that red book. It was as if the entire house had been brought down. She was still frantically searching for her mother's red diary.

"Where is it? Where is it?" she muttered to herself.

"I have to find it. I'm sure there is something in it," she said to herself.

She was in the basement opening drawers, shuffling through them, and throwing down old books on the floor.

She had dismissed the contents of a drawer when she saw something red out of the corner of her eye.

"Yes, I've found it," she nearly shouted.

She held the same diary in which her mother wrote that day.

"Yes...this is the one!" She opened the diary. It was in a torn and tattered condition. The cover was coming off, and the pages in it were loose.

On the first page was an illustration of the three family members: Richard, Grace, and Rachel. The words, "My Wonderful Family," were written just below the picture in beautiful handwriting. The picture made her smile. Lovingly, she moved her hand over the picture.

She turned the page. On the second page was a hand-drawn picture of the city welcome board; The City of Bridgeport and the words, "In this city, people lived in peace and harmony. We were all like one family, loving and helping each other. But all that changed one day. It changed when the dirty witch came to this city," were scrawled underneath in Grace's handwriting.

Rachel turned to the next page. "Rachel, this is for you. One day, when you grow up, this diary will answer all of your questions." Grace had written the message to Rachel on the next page all those years ago. The message continued.

"It was on a Saturday in March 1982 that I first saw her, the wicked witch, 'Maya.' Richard was off from work. We went for a drive with Rachel after the church. Richard got out of the car to buy candy for Rachel.

Suddenly, Richard saw a pickup truck come at a high speed. As the truck passed them, we noticed a weird-looking person sitting in the truck bed with a piece of cloth covering him. It was just odd.

Richard pointed at the truck and said, 'A little early for a joy ride, don't you think?'

And once they were back in the car, Richard put the police siren on and started to follow the pickup truck. Since Richard knew the city very well, he took a short cut in hopes that he could catch the truck.

Richard stood in the middle of the road waiting for it. The moment Richard saw the truck; he waved the driver to stop. The truck was being driven by a lady who had her face covered with a scarf. It was Maya.

'Ma'am, I'm hoping you don't want to kill anybody on this fine day, but at the speed you were going it's a hard assumption,' warned Richard.

'I am sorry officer. I am coming from Folsom. I didn't know the speed limits here,' Maya had replied in an irritated voice.

Richard took a round of the truck and looked at the license plate. He noticed Jerome sitting in the back. There seemed to be something heavy lying next to him. This was also covered with cloth. Jerome gave a blank look to Richard.

'What is in this?' Richard asked, but Jerome continued to give him a blank look.

Richard pulled the cloth to the side and realized that it was a casket.

Maya was watching everything from the rear view mirror.

'License and Registration, Ma'am,' Richard asked, moving towards the front side of the truck.

Maya started the truck and drove it away at a high speed.

Richard rushed back to his car and followed the truck. The police car reached the pickup. He honked at the horn but she didn't stop.

Maya started chanting. She looked at Richard's car following her through the rear view mirror. The moment she did, the front tires of his car burst and it swiveled badly.

It took some effort for Richard to stop the car without having an accident. He rushed out of the car and saw the truck driving away. Jerome was celebrating in the back of the truck."

Rachel continued to read. She could only vaguely remember this episode.

"'Richard was very disappointed. She wouldn't have driven off like that unless she had something to hide.' he thought.

It wasn't until three weeks later that we found out what was inside that casket. Once again, the three of us were driving. I clearly remember that Rachel was singing a poem for your dad. Your father noticed the same pickup truck parked on the roadside. He stopped the car and looked around. Nobody could be seen for a distance.

When your father used his binoculars, he saw Jerome walking towards an abandoned house. He instructed me to drive back home, promising me that he would soon be back. I tried to stop him, but he was determined to go. He drew out his gun and rushed towards the woods. Within a few minutes he was out of my sight.'

I decided to follow Richard. He had reached the abandoned house taking cover among the trees and bushes. He could see no one near the house. When we reached the house, he was standing near a window. I quietly slid close to him.

Through the window, we saw that there was a wooden casket lying in the room, and a man was lying in it. He was chained. Maya stood near him. I remember clearly that Maya was addressing the man in the casket as Willie and asking him if he was ready to quit his life as a vampire and join her in her world. She was telling the man in the coffin that worshipping Lehasha could give him unmatched pleasures. She told Willie that she knew how to bring Lehasha to the world. The man in the coffin refused to surrender his life to her evil gods. He begged her to free him and told her he did not want to be her slave.

Maya clearly declared that she would have her way one day, even if it meant waiting for years and years. They had a major argument. While Maya wanted him to accept life as her slave, he kept on insisting for his freedom.

Then, Maya pressed a silver chain to the man's body. Every place where the chain touched his body burned. Fangs appeared in his mouth, but he was unable to attack Maya.

Your father decided to face this lady. He pulled out his revolver and walked inside the house. I could see him through the window. I thought your father was crazy to fight with a vampire and a witch all by himself, with just one revolver in his hand.

Maya and Jerome looked angrily at him. Maya called herself a fool for having let him go just days earlier.

Before anything else happened, the man in casket started shouting at your dad to leave. He announced that she was a witch and it would not be easy to defeat her. Maya also asked your father to leave or to be ready to face consequences.

Richard decided to hold his ground. He kept the gun pointed at them and ordered them to lie on the floor. When they did not relent, he shot at Maya. The bullet missed her. She said a chant and the bullet came back towards your father. He was hit in the chest.

I rushed towards the car, lifted you and ran back for our lives. I did not want Maya to know that I had seen everything or that you are around this place. She would have killed us. I have never shared this with anyone. I was ready to die at her hands, but I did not want her to harm you in any manner.

Richard did not return that night. I knew he would not come back home. I knew I would not be able to answer your questions. After a few days, they found his car abandoned near a cliff. His body was never found. Nobody except me knew where he was."

Rachel kept reading the diary. Finally, she had answers to her lifelong questions. She reached the last page.

"The town was never the same again. Violence, crime, deaths are all that the city has seen since that day. No one is safe. Maya is an evil and cruel lady. I wonder how much harm she can do to this city and its people. She has ruined everything. There is not a single family that has not been affected by her deeds. I don't know who will punish her, and I wonder how and when all this will come to an end."

Rachel put the diary close to her chest. She thought about all the pain and agony that her mother had suffered by herself for all those years. She thought about all the members in Maya's group. Her thoughts ran in the direction of plans to relieve the town of that witch.

"I can, Mom, and I will. I want to do that for my daddy. I want do that for you. I want to do that for this beautiful town. And I want to do it for myself," said Rachel to herself. Suddenly, her face hardened with confidence. All the fears and apprehensions dissolved. She felt confident that she could face Maya.

After thinking for some time, she decided to face Jerome. She used her binoculars to observe him through the window. She saw that he was lying down on the ground. He didn't move from the spot for a long time. She decided to get a cup of coffee for herself. Once back from the kitchen, she again looked at Jerome using the binoculars. He plucked some leaves and fruits from the tree and ate them.

Eventually, he walked towards her house. As Rachel sees Jerome approaching the house she runs to the kitchen doors which faces the back of the house. Jerome sniffed around the place, behaving as if he thought she was not at home. Suddenly, he realized that she was standing near him. She motioned 'What?' to him, but he stared at her with a blank face. She gestured again, but he just continued to stare at her. They stood for minutes staring at each other.

Rachel pulled out a candy bar and extended it to him. He hesitated, but she pushed the bar a little further. He gathered some courage and took the bar. He immediately opened the wrapper and started to eat it. Once he was done with the bar, he ran to his lookout on the tree across the street.

Rachel had decided that she would follow Jerome the next time he came down from the tree.

Chapter XXXVII

The Truth

At Steve's funeral, mourners said prayers as the grave was prepared for his casket. Some people stood around it while Michael prayed, "From clay he came, he goes back to it. Oh Lord, please save the soul of your servant. In Jesus' name we pray. Amen."

I told you I didn't want to come here! I told you! You didn't listen, Daddy. I told you..." shouted Amy, crying all the while and reaching for where her father's body was being interred.

Rachel came running and stopped near the casket. She looked at Steve's face. Her mind was clouded with thoughts. One minute, she thought about her own father, and the next about Johnny and Amy. She thought of the first day she had met her childhood friend in the church and how happy she was. She remembered feeling that good days were about to come back to the town. "I was wrong. Nothing in this town is going to change. We are never going to see happiness," she repeated to herself over and over again.

Johnny continued to stare at the casket with a blank face. The pain that he felt at this moment was burning him from inside.

"Johnny, say goodbye. Come on, give him a last kiss," said Michael bending down on his knees close to Johnny.

The words "last" and "final" were a little too much for the young boy. He looked at his father's dead face, and tears starting rolling down his cheeks. Johnny remembered his father driving the car into the city, his reading the Bible to them, and playing with them.

His cries became louder.

"Daddy, don't go," shouted Johnny looking at his father's dead body.

"Daddy, please don't go. Please, don't go, Daddy!" said Johnny crying helplessly. There was nothing that he could do to raise his father, to stop him from his journey into another world. It was too much for him to cope.

The casket was closed and lowered into the grave. The soil was put on the grave. The children cried the whole time.

Michael held onto both children gently. Once the ceremony was over, he tried take them from the graveyard. As they were walking out, Johnny looked back and again started to cry loudly.

Rachel stood near the grave thinking about the children. There was nothing that she could do to ease their pain. Even though she had been through the same circumstances years before, she couldn't think of anything to offer these children that would make up for their circumstances. With her hands on her face, she started to weep. She looked around and saw the grave marking "Fr. Mario" nearby.

Rachel looked at the sky asking God when all of their misfortune and sorrow would stop. After a brief pause, she walked out of the graveyard. Briefly, she turned back to look at the grave and bid a final goodbye to her childhood friend.

Chapter XXXVIII

A Doom Laden Future

Ouso and Ben were on the mountain top. Ouso looked at the empty space for the sacrifice. His eyes traced the lines that started from each corpse and connected to form a dark thick line connecting to the place of the holy fire.

Ben walked towards Ouso and placed a wooden cross on the ground. He looked at Ouso and they both started to push it in the ground. Ben looked around at the circle and said to Ouso, "Just one more girl."

Ouso simply nodded his head. He was lost in deep thoughts. When he felt Ben still gazing at him, he said, "That is for the final virgin that concludes the ritual."

"Concludes? Then what?" asked Ben. He was surprised and curious.

"When the final ritual completes, the Lord Lehasha will be born," said Ouso as he continued pushing the wooden cross into the ground.

This amount of information was not sufficient for Ben. He had been associated with Maya for many years now, but had never been allowed to know her secrets.

"The evil god that Maya worships?" asked Ben in a cautious voice. He knew he was treading on a sensitive topic. Ouso had never so willingly answered his questions.

"Yes, from Maya's womb there at that spot," said Ouso pointing towards the center position where the blood marks connected.

He then pointed at the chained corpses and said, "These dead virgins, they will all come back to life that day. Maya said they will come back to serve Lehasha."

"All of them," said Ben looking at the dead corpses. He could feel his entire body twitching. Something was making him uncomfortable.

Chapter XXXIX

Another Grave

From the window of her house, Rachel kept an eye on Jerome hidden in the trees. She was sure that Jerome had an important role to play. She knew that he could provide a key to many hidden locks.

She noticed some movement on the tree. Jerome stepped down and started walking along the road towards the jungle. She rushed out of the house and decided to follow him.

Jerome stopped near a cluster of trees where a herd of goats was busy eating grass. Suddenly, they began to run helter-skelter. Jerome had nearly caught one of the goats, but it escaped. After lots of chasing, he caught one of them.

Mirroring her mother's actions from years ago, Rachel parked her car nearby and stealthily observed Jerome's activities. She saw him catch a goat and walk into the forest with it. As he moved on through the woods, Rachel followed him, hiding herself well behind the trees and bushes. She stopped when she saw Jerome tying the goat to a tree with a rope. Then he sat under the branches next to the goat.

The day was coming to an end, and night skies moved in. Back in the forest, Jerome sat near the goat. Rachel watched him from a distance. She felt exhausted and wanted to get back home. She heard the sound of an approaching car. Rachel checked her position wanting to make sure that she was not visible in the lights of the car. She noticed that Jerome stood up at his place and paced around restlessly.

The approaching car stopped near Jerome. With his head bowed, and without even looking at the person in the car, he lifted the goat and sat on the back seat. Once he was seated, the car drove away.

Rachel had been able to identify Maya and Tony in the car. Without switching on the headlights of her own car, she started following them from a distance.

After a few minutes' drive, the car stopped at the entrance of the woods. Tony and Maya stepped out of the car and Jerome followed them. He held the goat like it was his most prized possession.

Rachel parked her car at a distance from theirs. She stepped out, taking care not to make any noise.

The three of them had already started walking towards the woods unmindful of the fact that Rachel followed.

In the distance, Rachel could see a faint light. It seemed that they were headed in its direction. As she moved closer to the light, she realized that it was coming from a house. Even in darkness, it was not difficult to tell that the house was abandoned.

Rachel hid herself behind a tree and observed the group. It wasn't clear what they were doing, but she could make out that Maya said some chants while Tony held out the ball of light. After a few minutes, the three vanished inside. She was scared and held onto the cross in her neck.

Rachel's mind was suddenly clouded by a multitude of thoughts. Faces of her father, mother, Steve, Johnny, and Amy flashed through her mind. She felt strength come to her, and she decided to go inside.

Inside, Rachel saw a casket lying in the ground. While Maya and Jerome stood near it, Tony lit the lamps placed in the room.

Maya looked at Jerome, who bent down to open the casket.

It was minutes before William opened his eyes. After being in the dark for so many days, his eyes took some time to adjust to the lights. Even the slightest glimmer pained his eyes.

William looked at Maya blankly. Maya smiled at him in the hope that he would relent and join her. She was desperate to have him and wished he would give in.

Tony brought one of the lamps closer to Maya and the casket. Maya took the lamp from him and pointed it at William's face.

"There he is. Handsome as always! Hello, my sweet heart... Look at me. Let me see the changes these years have made." said Maya. She spoke like a lover proud of her mate. There was pride in her voice, but it was a twisted and sick think to be proud of.

William closed his eyes to the bright lights. Maya allowed her eyes to travel from William's face to his chest and all over his body.

"The same old William! Oh, but you look tired! 16 years isn't a long enough nap?" continued Maya.

William didn't respond. Even though Maya had not visited him all these years, he knew that she was there with some specific objective. Any resistance from his side was only going to make things worse for him. He knew Maya very well.

"Oh come on. It's me! Open your eyes, William. It is Maya, your sweetheart. Look at me. Talk to me," she cooed in a mocking, yet pleading, voice.

Rachel carefully walked in the direction from which the light was coming. She held onto the cross around her neck. She heard Maya say the name "William" again and again.

Rachel peeped in and quickly withdrew. Very carefully, she again tried to look through the slightly open doors and stressed her ears to hear the conversation taking place. She could hear only two voices--one she was sure was Maya's.

"Look at this. Look at my poor William. He is tired, hungry, and sick," said Maya looking at Jerome.

"Why does he look so pale, like he is dying? You don't feed him at all? That is so bad," continued Maya looking at Jerome.

Jerome was quick to break eye contact with Maya. He felt restless and started to pace the room.

Maya passed the lamp to Tony and bent down near the casket.

"Are you hungry, William? Do you want to feed on me?" asked Maya seductively. Touching her throat and moving closer to William, she showed him her neck.

"Come on Willie. This is your Maya. You can drink my blood. I am all yours. Come on. Drink from me," she said moving her face closer to William's face.

William turned his head and started to look away from her.

"See, this is your problem. You're stubborn. You don't listen. You don't obey," continued Maya.

Rachel was on the last step. She heard Maya's voice.

"It really doesn't matter, does it? Twenty years, fifty, is not going to make a difference in you. You had the option to choose to enjoy your life with me or live in captivity like this. You asked for this pain and you got it. It is your fault. You deserve it," spewed Maya with anger.

Rachel looked inside the room. She saw that Maya's face was very close to the casket. Rachel listened carefully and heard Maya say,"I could have killed you any time, William, but I kept you here. I kept you alive, because I love you."

William looked at Maya helplessly. He had started to lose his patience. He had no idea when it was going to end for him.

"All these years I waited for you, William. I thought one day you'd see reason. I don't want to keep you this way. I want you by my side, in my bed. We were so happy once," gushed Maya.

"I'm asking you for the last time. William, my vampire, do you want to spend your life with me?"

William looked at Maya anxiously. There was an uncomfortable silence in the room.

"Are you ready to forgo your vampire life and join us? Are you willing to accept and surrender to Lehasha?" her voice roared once again.

William chose silence.

Rachel was still watching everything from a crack in the door. She could hear everything clearly in the silent night. She was scared to imagine the extent to which Maya would go in her evil endeavors. It was the cross around Rachel's neck and the surety that her mother was with her that gave her the strength to continue spying in the abandoned house.

"Answer me William! Do you want to escape from darkness and spend your future with me? In return, I can offer you strength, eternity, and all the riches and pleasures of this world. Do you want a never-ending life with me?"asked Maya.

Once again, William did not utter a word and turned his head in the other direction.

"Can you really afford to say no again?" bargained Maya.

While Maya's complete demeanor at this moment spoke of the anger and lust that she felt for William, his demeanor showed his determination not to give in to her demands or his helplessness.

"Do you want me, William? Answer me." She commanded.

Without uttering a single word, he insulted Maya greater than any action he could take against her.

Maya bent down near the casket and moved her hand seductively on his chest.

William simply shook his head no and proceeded to close his eyes.

"Fine. So be it. I knew your answer. But I wanted to know if all these years had made any change in you. I see they haven't. Stubborn as ever." Maya stood.

"You are not going to get your freedom. You are going to die," promised Maya.

She pulled Tony in front of William and said, "I found someone better than you, and, with my help, he will be more powerful and stronger than you, too. When he's ready, I will come back...for the joys of watching him destroy you."

Maya signaled to Tony. He opened a bag and a cat jumped out of it.

Maya took the cat in her hands and began to caress it with love.

"In a few weeks, all your strength will be drained from you. All your vampire powers will be destroyed. Your mind and soul will be pulled from your body and will be passed to him." She gestured with the cat in her hands. "Your mind and soul will join inside Billy's body."

"Your body will die, but your soul and your mind, with all the good memories of our days together, will live in this cat's body forever, William."

William was shocked.

Seeing his face made Maya laugh aloud.

"No!" shouted William with his first words of the evening.

Maya stopped laughing and said, "You cannot defeat me, William. Nobody can."

William was worried. He hoped for death. He had always thought that refusing Maya would result in his death, not his eternal life of misery. "No, please, no. You can't do that. Kill me, and let me go of this world. Please," shouted William.

Jerome had a bewildered look on his face. He couldn't understand why William was pleading for death.

Rachel remained outside the room.

"You wanted to get out of that box? I'm granting your request. Your soul will live under my control forever is the price. I am not letting you go, William. I won't."

"But, you have the freedom to chase all the mice you want," she teased after a brief pause.

"No, no. Please no," pleaded William trying to make some sense with her.

Maya began laughing hysterically. She placed the cat near William's face. 'This is your future body, William, where you will spend the rest of your life," said Maya moving away from the casket.

The cat started to smell William and scratched his face. William cried out in pain. Blood oozed from the scratches.

"Billie, you stay here until dark moon day. You two get to know each other. After all, you'll be spending the rest of eternity together," said Maya talking to the cat.

William was in pain, and Jerome looked at his face.

Maya took out a square piece of silver metal from the pocket of her jacket. She raised it and stabbed it hard through William's hand.

William cried out.

"This is for rejecting me again. No one disrespects me. No one," she repeated while delivering a swift kick to the coffin.

Hearing Maya approaching the doorway, Rachel knew it was time to run.

Rachel turned back and slipped out of the house. She knew she had to save herself or Maya would kill her also. She could hear William's cries while running away. She ran quite a distance before hiding in the brush. She could still see the light from the abandoned house.

Maya walked out of the house with Tony following her closely. They had accomplished their goals with William.

In the house the cat was running here and there, and Jerome sat near the casket looking at William.

William looked completely exhausted. It had been so many days since he had eaten anything, and the ordeal with Maya drained him further. The cat scratched him all over, causing pain and irritation. The silver in his hand burned him, which was worse that the cat scratches. Tears rolled down his face.

Jerome's eyes were full of sympathy for William. He had seen the poor vampire lie in the casket endlessly for years. He picked up the cat and threw it out of the casket. Then, he pulled the silver from William's hands and threw it away.

The goat that Jerome had brought in let out a meek bleat reminding everyone of its presence. Jerome turned and picked it up. He brought it over to William, but William turned his face to the aside, denying his food. Instead of eating, he asked, "Will you do me a favor?"

In all these years this was the first time that William had spoken to him. Jerome looked at him a little confused for he had never expected that he could be of any use to William.

"Please, will you do me a favor?" asked William again desperately.

Jerome nodded. William looked at the silver rod nearby.

"Please, pick up that piece of silver and stab it through my chest. Push it through as hard as you can. Kill me."

Jerome was completely dumbfounded. He didn't know whether he should agree to what William was saying. He knew he could set him free from the casket; he could also set him free from his life, but the thought of what Maya would do sent jitters through his body.

The cat could sense the conversation between William and Jerome. It came and stood near the piece of silver and made a rough noise.

"Please, if you kill me, my life ends here. My soul will go in peace. I don't want to be controlled by that witch. I don't want my soul to be her slave forever. I can't have this pain anymore," said William.

Jerome again lifted the goat and placed it near William's face.

William shook his head in no, indicating that he did not want it.

"You fed me all these years. You are my only family in this world. I will be happy to die at your hands. Please, save my soul from her captivity. I beg you. Please, have mercy on me. Please."

Jerome looked back at William with helplessness written largely on his face.

William looked back in sadness.

Jerome replaced the lid of the casket, closing it once again.

"I know you're scared of Maya. Like me, you're just a slave to her. You have no life other than to obey what she commands you. You will live and die as her slave," said William through the closed casket.

"Please, kill me. Please, save my soul from her captivity. Please, don't go," he pleaded with Jerome once again, but Jerome had already walked out of the room, and the cat had perched atop the casket.

Chapter XL

The Chosen One

The air was very heavy. Maya and Tony stood at the top of the mountain. The city of Bridgeport was far below. Maya's pet crow circled the hill thrice and perched on a tree. They both looked at the empty space where the last corpse belonged.

"I am the chosen one to bring Lehasha's offspring to the world. I learned and followed every rituals in the sacred book of rituals," said Maya

Tony listened to her attentively. The dedication that he showed towards Maya was exemplary. He hung on to every word that she said and followed every instruction religiously.

"On the dark moon day, your body and veins will fill with the blood of Lehasha. His blood is precious. Even a drop is miraculous. You will feel his presence inside you. Your spirit and body need to be connected with me immediately," she continued after a brief pause.

Tony looked at Maya.

"With you as a medium, once our bodies are connected, our Lord's blood will pass to my body. Thus, the son of Lehasha will be born to this world through my womb," Maya said with excitement.

"Yes. I am the chosen one. I am the chosen one to become the mother of our Lord Lehasha. It is once in hundreds of years a human gets to be converted to one among us. I thought it would be William, but he chose his destiny. It is time to end his captivity. Before the birth of Lehasha, William should be put to rest forever," continued Maya looking at Tony.

"When Lehasha is born, all of them will open their eyes again." She gestured at the sacrificed girls. "Not as humans, but as spirits to serve Lehasha in his earthly journey," she said taking a few steps towards the final pyre place.

"On the dark moon day, the final girl will be sacrificed. She is the most important among all. It should be someone young and healthy who does not believe in evil spirits and visits places of worship. Someone who has not committed deadly sins. An innocent and spotless person."

Tony felt had no idea who this girl was where they are going to find her at such short notice.

"Where are we going to get someone like that in this town?" worried Tony.

Maya nodded her head rapidly as if she knew who that girl was supposed to be.

"I found the person. Jerome will bring Rachel," said Maya.

Tony was a little shocked to hear this. "Rachel?" he confirmed. "The new girl who came to the center?" asked Tony again.

Maya nodded her head.

Meanwhile, the people of Bridgeport were fast asleep. They had no idea that once again, the evil spirits had something planned for them.

Pure and innocent Rachel was fast asleep in her bed. The white light from the moon fell on her face, and she looked beautiful.

"Yes, she will be the final sacrificial lamb. She fills all of the requirements," said Maya in a determined voice.

"But there's something suspicious about that girl. Who is she? Who asked her to come to me? What does she want? I need to know more about her before we use her," continued Maya. She had been unable to read her thoughts. She knew that Rachel would be the best sacrifice, but there was definitely something about her that made Maya uncomfortable.

Unmindful of everything planned for her, Rachel smiled in her sleep and muttered, "Yes, Mom, I will. I will." While at the mountain top, Tony continued to listen to Maya attentively. He knew they could not afford to make a mistake.

"The coming days and events are very important. On dark moon day, your body will be connected to mine to conceive Lehasha in my womb. William will be killed and his soul captured. That evening, the girl will be sacrificed for the final ritual before Lehasha is born,"' explained Maya

Tony nodded.

In the distance, the city lights twinkled innocently, illuminating the lives of the unsuspecting townspeople about to be used, once again, for Maya's evil.

Chapter XLI

The Fallen Guard

The sun had started to rise on the horizon. Jerome, asleep under the trees in front of Rachel's house, woke to the sun falling on his face. He looked around with a look of gloomy upon his features. He was lonely. His first thoughts after waking up were about William.

Rachel had been observing Jerome from her window since she woke up a little earlier. She gathered her courage and walked across the street to him. They both stood looking at each other. Jerome was taken aback by Rachel's presence. He knew she should be scared of him.

Rachel too was surprised by her mettle. She expected Jerome to hurt her, but he chose to stand still and look at her. Reaching into her pocket, Rachel drew out two candy bars. Extending her arm, she offered them to him. Jerome took the candy. She smiled at him and turned to walk back home.

He ripped open the wrappers and fed on the candy bars. He continued to sit under the trees and watch Rachel's window. William's words haunted his mind."You fed me all these years. You are my only relative in this world. I will be happy to die at your hands. Please, save my soul from her captivity. I beg you."

Then, he thought of everything that Maya had said to William." Your captivity and vampire life will be over, but your soul will be in the body of Billie, under my control forever."

William, Maya, and Tony's faces moved in front of his eyes. Suddenly, all the faces were replaced by one - Rachel's. Yes, she had replaced all.

Chapter XLII

Dawn

In the afternoon, Rachel came out of her house. Jerome still sat under the tree, unmindful of the sun falling on him. They both exchanged glances. Rachel smiled at him but he didn't respond. Continuing out of her house, she got in the car and began driving out of the town.

She checked in the back view mirror if Jerome had got up to follow her. To her surprise he sat still without moving.

Rachel parked the car at the edge of the cliff and looked ahead. "Mom, dad, that witch killed Steve. The church will never open again. Maya is going to kill that vampire. She's going to be more powerful now. I don't know why, but she has sent somebody to follow me. I'm not scared to die, but I am worried for this city. I don't know what is going to happen. I don't know what to do," thought Rachel. As always, she was confident that they would answer her questions. They had always been there with her.

"Dad, Mom, can you hear me?" asked Rachel aloud. Her voice resonated. "I love you. And I miss you...miss you both so much!" she shouted. The echo of her love made her smile.

Rachel started her car and drove back home. She saw that Jerome was still sitting under the same tree.

Chapter XLIII

The Past

For a change, Jerome didn't notice Rachel come back. He was lost in his own thoughts, seeing everything but completely unaware.

Rachel noticed that Jerome was preoccupied. She watched from the window.

He thought about his life. His past played like a movie in front of him. He remembered himself wandering around the streets as a little boy. He was an orphan who often fed on food from the trash bins. There were times when he would resort to snatching purses from women and pick-pocketing. The day he had seen Maya crossing the road, her red purse caught his attention. He followed her and, at the first opportunity, snatched the bag and ran away. He was caught by some people walking along the street.

Maya asked the people to leave him. When the crowd subsided, she began talking to him. She asked him his name and why he wasn't in school.

After knowing that he was an orphan, and that he had no one to take care of him, she had asked if he would like to run errands for her. Maya took him home where he met William for the first time.

Everything was very nice until one day when Maya and William had an argument. He could make out that William wanted to leave while Maya was trying to stop him. William seemed determined to go. To prevent him, Maya said a spell which rendered William unable to move from his place.

He saw that Maya had tied William with chains, and after a few days, the casket arrived, and William was put inside it.

Another morning, Maya instructed him to clean the garden and went out. When she came back, there was a pickup truck following her. She called out for him to help her move the casket to the pickup truck. She instructed him to sit in the truck while she drove to the abandoned house in the forest.

There, she put the casket in the room and instructed him to take care of William. "Once every week, you have to bring him a goat. Without opening his chains, just place the goat near his face."

William and Jerome looked at each other.

Jerome's thoughts moved to days earlier. He remembered how William pleaded for freedom. "Please, save my soul from her captivity. I beg you. I know you are scared of Maya. She is using you. You are just a slave to her. Once I die, she will abandon you. She won't need you anymore." He could still hear William's voice. In all these years, it was the first time that William had pleaded like that.

Jerome's expression changed. From helplessness and sadness, he seemed to have cleared his thoughts and made his up mind. He rose from his place, took a deep breath, and left to take action. After some while, he returned with a goat and tied it to the tree.

Once the sun had set, he picked up the goat and ran to the forest. Rachel observed everything. The moment Jerome picked up the goat and ran, Rachel rushed out of the house. She knew where he was going and decided to follow him in her car.

Jerome reached the abandoned house. He opened the door and entered the room with the grave. He placed the goat on the floor. He wiped a mixture of tears and sweat from his face. He didn't want to lose the only relative he had. He rushed to open the casket.

William was surprised to see him. He looked at him confused. For a minute William thought that Maya was with him. He looked around and realized that Maya was not there.

Jerome started to pull at the chains in order to free William from the casket. He succeeded in breaking nearly all the chains except the ones around William's hands and feet. Every time he pulled at the chain, it spewed fire burning William making it difficult for Jerome to break it.

Rachel reached the entrance of the house and rushed to the room. She was confused upon seeing what was happening in the room. Time and again, a fire would emit. She moved closer to Jerome and William, wanting to see what was happening.

She saw that Jerome was trying to break open the locks on the chain. Every time he hit the lock or pulled at the chain, another fire would flare. The cat moved around the room making weird and angry sounds.

After a lot of effort, Jerome was able to slip William out of the casket. William's hands and feet were Jerome started to drag William towards the door, but the cat got in their way. He pushed it aside. The cat jumped on a table and, from there, it charged at them with anger.

Jerome tried to help William move in the other direction, but once again the cat blocked their way. It pounced at Jerome, who closed his eyes. William lay on the floor watching all the commotion. There was nothing that he could do.

Jerome opened his eyes to loud sounds being made by the cat. He saw Rachel beating it with one of the flower vases lying in the room. The cat made a pained sound. Jerome felt encouraged to see the cat expertly handled by Rachel. He rushed towards William to help him stand up.

Rachel had dealt with the cat by this time. It lay half dead on the floor. She ran towards Jerome and William. While Rachel held onto William, Jerome tried to pull at his chains, but to no avail. Every attempt to free William meant getting burnt.

William cried out in pain. Looking to Jerome he said, "I'm thirsty. I need to feed or I'm going to die."

Rachel signaled Jerome to stop. She took out a pin from her shirt and started to fiddle with the locks. After a few tries, she opened the locks restraining William's hands. She signaled him to sit on the floor and started working with the locks binding his feet.

Jerome brought the goat near William, who looked at the goat desperately.

William was worried that he would scare Rachel, but he had no alternative. He had to use his fangs for drinking blood. If he did not feed on something, he would soon be dead. He took the goat in his hands and allowed his fangs to come out of his mouth. He started sucking at the goat.

Rachel looked up and saw William feeding on the goat.

After drinking, William dropped the goat on the floor. By this time Rachel had managed to open the remaining locks.

William looked energized. He took a few deep breaths and smiled at Rachel and Jerome. They each held him by an arm and the three made their ways outside.

They reached the car.

Rachel opened the back door of the car, and Jerome helped William to get in. She opened the passenger side door wanting Jerome to take the seat. To her surprise, he shook his head frantically saying, "No."

"Come on, come with us," said Rachel persuading him to join them.

Jerome shook his head again. He started to push Rachel towards the car. He desperately wanted her to leave and get to safety.

She didn't want to leave him there. She knew that Maya would treat him badly.

"Please, take care of yourself," said Rachel while sitting in the driver's seat.

She switched on the ignition and drove away.

Jerome watched the car move away. He went pale thinking about Maya. He knew she would not take his escape lightly. He sat on the ground with his head in his hands.

Rachel had no idea where to take William. She knew wherever they went Maya would find them. She looked at William in the back seat. He looked tired and in great pain. "You okay?" she asked.

William nodded his head.

Rachel decided that it would be best to hide William in the basement of her own house.

It was hard for William to walk down the steps of the basement all by himself. Rachel helped him move down.

They reached the basement. He turned his face towards her and said, "I am so thirsty."

Rachel was confused. She had no idea what this man wanted. She helped him sit on a board lying on the floor and took the place next to him. "I'm tired. I think I'm dying," he said.

She took off her coat, looked at his face, and offered, "You can drink my blood."

William looked at her throat and then her face. He wondered why this girl was offering herself to him. He was worried for her.

"It's ok. You can feed on me. I can handle it," she said looking at William reassuringly.

William looked at her throat. He hesitated because he didn't want to harm her. "What if I take too much blood?"

"There's no choice. Just do it," said Rachel, showing her throat to him again.

William's fangs appeared, and he turned towards her. He started to suck blood from her throat. She closed her eyes as she felt sharp pain. Her hands gripped William's arm. As he continued to feed on her, she felt the pain rise. To brace herself, she dug her nails into his skin. He realized that he was draining her. She had gone pale. He pulled away.

Rachel was relieved. She stood up and took a few deep breaths rapidly.

William looked at her, worried that she still looked pale.

"I'm, I'm sorry... I was so thirsty. I didn't mean to take so much, "he apologized.

"I think you almost killed me," said Rachel as she turned towards him and caressed her throat.

"I thought I was going to die," she repeated after a brief pause.

"I... I just lost control. I forgot where I was," said William.

"That's okay. I understand. I'm glad you're okay now," said Rachel shrugging her shoulders.

It was silent enough to hear a pin drop. Rachel took a look at the wounds and burn marks and asked, "Do you need a doctor?"

William shook his head "No... A human doctor won't be able to do much. I just need some rest," he said.

Rachel nodded. "I'll be right back." Saying this, she went to the ground floor of her house. In the bathroom, she opened a drawer. She took out some ointment and went back to the basement. She motioned for William to sit on the plank. She put the medicine on his chest and hands then covered them with a bandage.

William cried out in pain.

"The sun will be up soon. You can sleep here. I will come back for you tonight," said Rachel after applying the medicine.

The moment William lay on the ground and closed his eyes, he felt asleep.

Rachel closed the door of the basement and walked up the stairs.

Chapter XLIV

The Communion

Inside Maya's center, Ben played the flute.

A fire burned, and Maya and Tony sat in front of it naked.

Maya sat with a prayer book in her hands. She read aloud from it in a foreign language.

At a certain point in the prayers, Ouso began to play the drums.

Maya threw a white powder in the air. Some powder fell in the fire, and it flared higher. She chanted her mantras reverently.

Tessa was decorating the bed with white and red flowers. She lit the lamps on the bed posts. The room smelled strongly of the flowery fragrance.

Maya stopped chanting. She circled the fire and stood where she had started. She brought her hands together forming a cup, and a ball of fire appeared. She threw it at Tony, and his entire body started to glow.

Complete silence overtook the room. Tessa tip-toed around the fire to stand next to Ouso.

Maya resumed her prayers. This time, her voice was like a deep hum.

Ouso signaled Tessa to lift a clay jar. She raised it and walked towards Tony. She poured the entire contents of the jar over his head.

"This is the precious blood of Lehasha that passes through your body," said Maya.

The blood dripped over Tony's body. Wherever the blood touched his body, his flesh returned its natural color.

"This blood prepares you for the Lord," said Maya.

The blood reached his feet, and Tony stood still in a pool of it.

Tessa placed the jar in Tony's hands, and then he drank a few sips of the blood before giving the jar back to her. She placed it on the table and moved back to her position next to Ouso.

Ouso signaled Ben, who stopped playing the flute and walked up to a wooden box nearby. He opened the lid and let the snake slide out. He moved back to his original position and played a flute.

The snake crawled up to the jar of blood and began drinking it. After the snake had finished, it crawled out of the jar and danced to the music. Within minutes, it started to crawl towards Tony. It reached Tony and slithered over his entire body before reaching his throat. Ouso played a drum roll while Ben got back to his flute. The snake bit Tony on the throat. He closed his eyes to the pain.

The snake wrapped its body around Tony's neck. The snake pours Lehasha's blood from its mouth into the wounds on Tony's throat. The blood passes through his veins. Tony's body began to glow as the blood pass through it.

Once the blood had reached every part of Tony's body. The snake crawled down from his neck. At Tony's feet, it swayed to the music before slithering away towards the fire. The snake slid itself into the fire.

Ben and Ouso stopped playing the music.

Maya chanted mantras for a long time, and then tossed the white powder in throughout the room and into the fire, which flared. She closed the book and walked towards Tony seductively. She stood in front of Tony admiring the blood dripping from his body. The veins in Tony's body took on a dark blue color. They glittered in the light of the fire.

Ben started to play the music once again, and Ouso approached Maya and Tony. "This body has the sacred blood of the master," said Ouso. He took their hands and joined them

Ouso went to Maya and Tony and took Tony's right hand. He pulled Maya's right hand and placed it on Tony's announcing, "With this you are connected to Lehasha."

Maya looked at Tony's body. Her face became wild. She moved forward and placed her lips on his. Overcome with passion, she bit his lips and touched the blood over his body, licking the blood from her fingers.

"This is the blood of the Lehasha. Your skin, the veins in your body, is filled with the blood of our Lord. It is powerful and precious," said Maya licking his face. She bit his throat right at the place of snake marks. She sucked blood from his throat. She looked all over his body with eyes full of lust and desire.

"I want Lehasha's blood inside me, in my womb," demanded Maya, holding Tony's hand and guiding him towards the bed.

Making him lie down on the bed, she licked the blood from all over his body. Feeling the passion for Tony's body, she scratched him all over until blood dripped. Her hands and face travelled down between his legs, and he closed his eyes in pleasure.

Tony took a deep breath and, ignoring his painful scratches and the snake bite, he pulled her on top to bite her lips tenderly. He turned and placed Maya under him. He was ready. He thrust his manhood into her softness. He pushed himself into her while she pounded under him harshly.

Tony was excited and high. He pushed himself in and out of Maya, and she licked his shoulders. He found it difficult to control both the pleasure and pain that he was experiencing at the same time.

Ouso and Ben continued to play the music while Tessa watched Maya and Tony make love.

Suddenly, Ouso stopped playing the drums and took a few quick steps towards the bed. His eyes were darting again and again towards the door. Maya and Tony had ignored his initial movement, but they could not ignore his close vicinity.

Tony, who was on the verge, stopped. Maya looked at Ouso with irritation and anger.

Ouso pointed towards the door. The cat stood in the doorway bleeding. The moment Maya looked in that direction, it collapsed.

Maya pushed Tony aside and rushed out of bed. She went to stand next to her cat. It didn't take her long to understand what had happened. She started shouting William's name in rage.

Chapter XLV

Awakening

In the basement of Rachel's house, William lay fast asleep on the floor.

He suddenly felt as if someone was calling out his name. Opening his eyes, he sprung up. "Who is it," he asked suspiciously. He wanted to identify who was present in the room.

He didn't see anyone. Between the voice and the new environment, he was very confused. "Where am I," thought William.

He heard a door open and looked in that direction to find Rachel walking in. He was reminded of the events the previous day. William was relieved to be free from captivity.

Rachel helped him stand up.

He moved around the room a little before sitting on the floor again. He looked relaxed and healed.

"Fresh air feels amazing," said William taking a few deep breaths.

"Thank you," he said after a brief pause. Then he took the bandages off of his body.

"Healed in such a short time?" asked Rachel quizzically at him .

"Yes. Our bodies do that. The wound just heals itself," said William.

They were silent for a few seconds. William looked at her face.

"I don't know why you risked your life for me, but I am very thankful. I'll never forget this. Thank you," said William looking at her.

Rachel smiled back in reply.

"I'm sorry. I'm William. I don't know your name," said William.

Before Rachel could say anything, he said, "And I am a vampire." He looked straight in her eyes to gauge her reaction.

"I'm Rachel," she replied with a nod. She touched the bite marks on her throat.

"Oh, right. Sorry, but thank you," said William.

She extended her hand towards him and they shook hands.

"What year is this?" asked William.

"2014," replied Rachel.

"Wow. I was gone a long time... like 16 years. Feels good to be back," said William taking a deep breath. The long years of captivity flashed before his eyes. He stretched his arms as if trying to confirm that he was not bound by the chains.

"I know," said Rachel.

William was silent for a few minutes as if he heard something again. He signaled Rachel to be quiet and cupped a hand behind his ear to listen more closely. He looked at Rachel. There was suddenly an expression of panic on his face.

"I have to leave now. The witch knows I escaped and she will be looking for me. She's probably already found Jerome by now," said William.

Rachel could sense the gravity of the situation, but didn't have complete understanding.

"She may come here any time. Let me leave," said William.

"I'm not sure, but I think I understand," said Rachel.

William sniffed around the room.

"My smell is all over the place. She'll know I was here," said William pointing at the floor where he had slept.

"Scrub everything. Put garlic and cloves here and all over the house," instructed William.

He started to leave the house. He turned and looked at her throat. He bit his hand and, without giving Rachel an opportunity to understand what was happening, he put his blood on her bite marks. Within a few seconds, the marks disappeared.

"Your scars have gone," said William smiling at her.

"Thanks" said Rachel.

"Maya is going to be mad if she finds out it was you. You may want to disappear for a little bit. I suggest that you go stay with your family," said William walking up the stairs. Rachel followed him closely.

"It's just me. I don't have any relatives," said Rachel quite casually.

William turned to look at her. He wondered what this young girl would do with her life all alone. He briefly touched her shoulder to comfort her and said, "Be careful. Thank you for all your help."

"I don't want you to come out of the house with me. I hope we can meet again," said William standing on the last step.

Rachel nodded her head.

William rushed out of the house.

Even though Rachel didn't have complete understanding of Maya, she knew that she could be cruel and ruthless. She felt scared and worried for herself, William, and Jerome.

Chapter XLVI

Enmesh

Just outside the abandoned house in the woods, Jerome's body hung from a tree.

William reached the house and saw Jerome's dead body swaying. He noticed Maya's car leaving towards the city.

Back at home, Rachel had done exactly as William had told her. She had scrubbed the basement well and put garlic at different places in the house.

Late in the evening, she sat on a chair praying with the cross around her neck. She wondered where William was and what he was doing.

Her thoughts were broken by the ringing of the doorbell.

She sat up in her chair. For a flash of a second, she thought that William was back. She rushed to the main door.

On opening the door she was surprised to see Maya and Tony standing at the door.

"Hi Maya! What a surprise!" said Rachel after regaining her composure.

Maya chose not to speak, but to look straight into Rachel's eyes to read her thoughts.

Without waiting for Rachel to ask them to come inside, Maya walked towards the living room, and Tony followed her closely.

Maya sniffed hard as if trying to smell for something.

"Garlic?" thought Maya shaking her head and looking at Rachel questioningly.

"Is there something wrong?" asked Rachel

Tony gave her an angry look and signaled her to be quiet. Maya walked into the other rooms looking and sniffing around. Rachel followed them through the rooms.

"Why do all the rooms smell like garlic?" asked Tony.

"Oh, I was cooking dinner," replied Rachel with a smile.

Tony shook his head. He didn't believe her. Maya, by this time, had reached the basement. She opened the door and stopped after two steps. She sniffed hard and thought, "I'm sure he was here."

She rushed up the stairs, walked straight to Rachel, and asked in an authoritative voice, "Where is he?"

Composing herself, she asked, "Who?"

This was enough to send Maya over the edge. "Don't play with me. I know you saved William. Where is he now?" she shouted.

Rachel did not reply.

"Answer me. Where is he?" she commanded.

"I don't know," Rachel replied, shrugging her shoulders.

Maya looked at Rachel angrily. Everything played before her eyes. She saw Rachel hitting the cat with a flower vase, opening William's locks, and driving him away. She also saw William sleeping on the floor in the basement and leaving in the morning.

Maya couldn't control herself and slapped Rachel hard on the face with her full strength.

It was a little too much for the petite Rachel, who fell on the ground. The pain resulted in tears flowing from her eyes.

"Don't ever lie to me," screamed Maya bending down. She pulled Rachel by the hair.

"I know he will come back for you," said Maya. She pushed Rachel towards Tony.

Tony put her over his shoulder and walked out of the house.

Rachel tried to escape, but Tony held her tightly.

Maya opened the car trunk, and Tony threw Rachel inside.

Chapter XLVII

Face Off

Tony drove the car towards the abandoned house in the woods. He parked the car right in front.

Maya stepped out and stormed inside.

Tony opened the car trunk and pulled out Rachel. He again threw her over his shoulders and started walking towards the house.

Maya went straight to the room in which the casket lay. She kicked at the casket frantically in anger. "William! I will bring you back here. But next time, I won't waste time with this casket," she said.

Tony had reached the room with Rachel hanging over his shoulder. He put her on the ground and tied her hands to a wooden post.

After night fell, Tony lit the lamps while Maya chanted her mantras in front of the fire.

The house was surrounded by darkness. Outside, a fierce wind blew. A fox howled far away in the forest.

Maya stopped chanting and looked around. She stood right in front of Rachel.

Rachel was pale with fear.

"William, I know you are close by. I can smell you. I know you can hear me," said Maya hissing.

"I have her. I know you'll come to save her," continued Maya after a brief pause.

Maya chanted some mantras and a silver sword with wooden handles appeared in her hand. She threw it towards Tony.

"You couldn't save Jerome. Now, she will die, also, "Maya announced strongly.

Tony walked towards Rachel and placed the sword to her throat.

"You're not smart enough to run away, William. This girl will pay the price for your betrayal. She will pay the price for crossing me," continued Maya.

The sound of mantras being chanted could again be heard in Maya's voice. Her voice echoed in the dark, quiet night.

Maya and Tony missed the sound of dried leaves crackling amongst the sounds of the chants and wind.

Yes, somebody was walking towards the house.

It was only when the footsteps reached the main door that Tony heard them. He walked out towards the main door. Outside, he saw a goat running from one direction to the other.

Tony walked towards the goat wanting to determine if it was William. Upon not seeing anyone, he turned back. Before he could reach the first step, he felt a kick in his face. He let out a cry. Looking around, he could see no one.

Tony hadn't yet recovered from the earlier blow when he received a kick in his abdomen. He fell on the ground with the sword falling at a distance. He was sure that it was William who was hitting him. He scrambled to his feet to pick up the sword and stand up. He swung the sword around in the air.

"Come out whoever you are. Fight me face to face, you coward! I will show you my strength, then," shouted Tony.

William appeared behind Tony. He snapped his fingers wanting to catch Tony's attention.

Tony turned and saw William. He rushed to attack him and shouted, "You son of a bitch."

William stepped to the side and kicked Tony on his shoulder. He once again lost grip over the sword.

Tony ran empty-handed towards William, and they both got involved in a fight.

It was some time before William was able to overpower Tony. He threw Tony on the ground and sat over him. He grabbed Tony's head and twisted his neck.

Chapter XLVIII

A Deal

Maya stood in front of the fire chanting, unmindful of all the fighting outside. She had a wild expression on her face. Her skin looked dark and her eyes blood shot. She wasn't aware of Tony's absence. She threw the white powder and the fire flared higher.

Rachel stared at Maya terrified.

"Let the power of the universe fill this room. Let the power of light and darkness fill this room. Let the power that can control fill this room," Maya prayed.

Maya spoke in a foreign language. A swirl of wind entered the room, and the lamps began to flicker.

Suddenly, Tony's body was thrown at Maya from outside. She stopped chanting and opened her eyes. She was unable to complete her chant and had to stop her prayers.

On seeing Tony's body, Maya screamed out William's name and clenched her fists, digging her nails into her palms until they bled.

Maya closed her eyes. She stretched out her hand, and a sword appeared in her hand.

Turning towards Rachel, she said, "You helped him escape. You will face the consequence now," and she threw the sword towards her.

Rachel cowered and closed her eyes. She let out a cry in anticipation.

Suddenly, Grace appeared near Rachel and caught the sword midway.

Rachel opened her eyes to the sound of the sword falling on the ground, but she was unable to see Grace. She looked at the sword and then Maya.

This enraged Maya all the more. "You," she said, pointing towards Grace.

Rachel could not make out to whom Maya was talking.

Richard appeared at Maya's side. She was quite startled to see him there.

"What is happening? Didn't I kill you already?" Maya shouted.

"You killed my body, but you couldn't touch my soul. Let my daughter go," said Richard.

Maya turned towards Rachel and pointed in her direction.

Rachel didn't know what was happening. She could neither see anyone, nor hear anyone, but Maya seemed to be talking to people.

"Your daughter? So this was revenge?" exclaimed Maya.

"It's nothing. You deserve to be treated worse," said Richard.

"You cannot hurt our daughter. Whatever spells you have, whatever powers you possess, whoever your masters are, we will not let you hurt our daughter," said Grace with determination.

"Dad? Mom? Are you here?" said Rachel.

Maya looked at Grace.

"Harm our daughter and you will never know another moment's peace.   We'll haunt you night and day," threatened Grace.

Maya closed her eyes and started to say a spell. A new sword much bigger in size appeared in her hands.

"You can't threaten me. I can burn your soul," retorted Maya.

"You can burn us for a thousand years, but you'll never be free. Day and night, we'll be here," said Richard.

Rachel looked. Still, she couldn't see anyone. She looked at Maya, who seemed to be staring at nothing in anger.

"All we want is to save our daughter. Let her go," said Grace. Her voice was like the roar of a lioness standing in defense of her cubs. She moved in front of Rachel completely covering her.

"My daughter did no harm to you. You killed her father and sabotaged our life. All we ask is for you to let her go now," said Grace.

Maya shifted her gaze from Grace to Rachel and back to Grace.

"If I let her go, she leaves forever. I don't want her meddling in my affairs ever again," said Maya bargained with Richard.

"The next time I see her, I will end her forever," she continued.

Richard gave his assent by nodding his head while Grace said, "All right."

"But remember, we will be watching, Maya," said Richard.

"As long as you're silent," said Maya pointing towards Rachel.

Rachel looked around in the hope of catching a glimpse of her mother and father. Still, she could see no one.

Suddenly, Rachel felt a wet kiss on one of her cheeks. Richard walked towards Rachel and kissed her on the forehead. Both Richard and Grace had tears flowing down their cheeks.

Rachel began to cry. She knew that her parents were with her, and they had protected her from the evil Maya. It was bittersweet for her. Even though they didn't exist in the physical world any longer, her parents were there to protect her, to take care of her, from all dangers.

Maya walked out of the room with the sword in her hand and shouted for William.

Chapter XLIX

The Battle

Maya rushed outside to take revenge on William. He had not only killed Tony, but had wasted her continuous efforts of all these years. It had never been easy to get slaves, find virgins for the sacrifice, or please Lehasha.

As she stepped out, a rope fell from the air tying her hands. The sword in her hand fell on the ground.

Maya looked up and saw William on the roof. Angry, she tried to escape, but William was too powerful for her. All the rage and inconveniences made her blood boil. Her face was blood red. William quickly tied the rope with some bars protruding from the roof.

Maya realized that she would not be able to free herself. She closed her eyes and started to chant.

William quickly moved to tie her mouth in order to stop her chanting.

Maya opened her eyes and started shaking her entire body frantically.

William opened a leather bag and took out a needle and thick skein of thread from it. He started sewing Maya's mouth. Blood dripped from the wounds that the needle made. Maya could do nothing except writhe in pain.

William finished stitching her mouth and stood in front of her. "Now you are the one that is powerless. How does that feel?" he asked. He picked up Maya's sword and placed it to her throat.

Maya stood still. She knew that the slightest movement would be fatal for her.

William walked around her before taking a leap to the roof top.

Maya heaved a sigh of relief thinking that William had left.

Within seconds, the sword returned back to her throat. "Try attacking me again and see what I do with you." William hollered jumping down in front of her.

Maya knew that William was serious. She knew he would take revenge for all the torture to which she had subjected him. She was scared because William knew her ways well.

William bent down and put Maya's feet in chains. "Do you remember the first day you chained me, darling?" he asked.

"You've controlled this city long enough, Maya. You toyed with enough people's lives. Now look what you have done to this town. You've ruined it. Everything that you touch gets destroyed. Every place you set foot gets burnt. Think of the innocent lives you sabotaged. You killed for your pleasures and evil rituals. It is payback time," he continued.

Maya looked towards the city. The darkness had nothing to give her.

Rachel, who was still tied to the wooden post, couldn't see anyone around. She knew something was wrong; neither Tony nor Maya had returned. She pulled at her chain frantically.

Chapter L

The Protector

William walked into the house.

He saw Rachel standing with her hands tied. It was clear that she was extremely scared. He pulled out the cloth that had been stuffed in her mouth and started opening her chains.

Rachel started crying with relief. Having William's help made her feel as if there was someone from her family standing near her. The moment her hands were freed, she hugged him.

"Don't worry. Nobody will hurt you again," said William. He wanted to caress her hair, but resisted.

Once Rachel was a little composed, he looked deep into her eyes and asked, "Are you okay? I was getting worried that I might be too late."

Rachel was in no position to speak. She simply nodded her head.

"You need to leave immediately and go straight to your house. I have some unfinished business here," said William.

He took her hand and walked her towards the main door.

"Maya is still alive," he said without turning back. He was in a hurry.

The moment Rachel heard this, she stopped.

William again nudged at her hand, pulling her, and said, "Don't worry. She cannot hurt you again. Go home."

Rachel nodded and rushed outside.

"I will meet you soon," said William.

Rachel stopped and looked at his face for a moment. She nodded once more and ran out. In the porch area, she saw Maya tied to the roof.

Maya saw Rachel escaping. Her last hope of controlling William was also lost.

Chapter LI

Vengeance

Inside the abandoned house, William set the casket back in the grave.

He walked outside and stood in front of Maya.

"You never expected it to end like this, did you Maya? An end in which you have no control, totally powerless and painful," said William.

Maya looked at him angrily. She opened her eyes wide and made loud, gruff sounds. There was nothing else she could do.

"I could kill you right now, Maya. I could finish you forever. But, if I do that, you will just go in the blink of an eye without feeling any pain and suffering. But, that is not what I want. I want you to know the pain and suffering I had all these years while you caged me alive in that casket. I don't want you to die that fast. I want you to suffer and die," continued William.

He paused for a second and looked at her eyes.

Maya shook her body vigorously and pushed hard with all her force. She still hoped that all this shoving around and pushing will help her gain freedom.

William hit Maya very hard on the face, breaking her nose into a bloody mess.

Maya passed out, and William used this opportunity to untie her hands and throw her over his shoulder.

He got her inside the house and into the room of the grave. He threw her in the casket.

With the needle and the skein of thread, he stitched both hands together. All the pricking caused to her to awake from her unconsciousness.

"You kept me captive for years. I'm going to show you the same courtesy. I am keeping you captive hoping it will give you the time to look back at yourself, to think of all the bad things you have done, and repent for everything. That is my punishment for you," said William.

Maya lay in the casket crying out in pain. She could see the blood oozing out from her hands and falling all over her.

William looked around the room for the chains and locks with which he had been tied. He used the chains and the locks to chain Maya's body to the casket. He took one last look at her before closing the casket.

"I hope I never see you again, but if someday you come out of this hole and try to find me, I'll be prepared, and I will be waiting," said William with a kick at the casket. He lifted Tony's body over his shoulder and walked out of the house.

William stopped at the door of the room without even looking to bid his final goodbye. "I wish I could have made things worse for you." He closed the room and the slab of concrete.

Standing outside of the house, William knew what he wanted to do with Tony's body. He could hear the howling of a fox far away. He threw Tony's body on the ground at the edge of the woods. The fox immediately came to feed on it. It howled and was soon joined by many foxes.

Chapter LII

The Battle Continues

William walked away from the abandoned house in the forest. Not once did he look back at the house. He reached Maya's Paradise and walked in with a can of petroleum in his hands.

Within, he saw the various statues and snake boxes lying in the house. He collected them all and put them on the floor. He ventured into other rooms and brought down all the books and equipment used for prayers. It took some effort to locate Maya's main prayer book.

He opened the can and poured the petroleum over the pile of books, statues, and animals in the center of the floor. He took out a match box from his pocket and, with it, ignited the junk. They immediately caught fire. The flames spread.

The fire spread, forcing William out of the house.

William walked away from the house. The house flared behind him and could be seen even from far.

The fire had spread everywhere. The statues cracked under the heat. The books and all equipment were devoured by the fire. **But the space surrounding the main prayer book formed a circle and didn't burn.**

Chapter LIII

The Return

It was evening, and the sun was setting in the far west.

Rachel sat on a sofa in her living room. Her mother's wheel chair lay close by. There were a few boxes on the floor in the room. She stood up, looked at her watch, and stared outside the window. Saying, "Oh, the sun..." she smiled. Her thoughts drifted to William. It had been quite a few hours since she left him in the woods, and she was getting worried about him.

She went into her bedroom and quickly threw a few clothes in a duffel bag. She came to the living room and picked up her parents photograph and put in the bag. Back in her room, she thought of other things to gather.

Unexpectedly, she heard the sound of the doorbell. For a minute, William's name flashed in her mind. She rushed towards the main door.

Rachel opened it and saw William standing at the entrance. He smiled at her and she smiled back.

"Were you scared?" asked William.

"Oh, no... I slept all day. I just woke up," said Rachel. She realized that William was still standing outside as she stood in the doorway. She stepped back and asked William to come in.

As William stepped in and saw the duffle bag, he was a little surprised and asked, "Bags? Are you going somewhere?"

Rachel smiled back and nodded her head. "Yeah... Apparently the spirits of my parents appeared and made a deal with Maya on my behalf. I leave town, and I get to keep breathing," said Rachel.

William laughed and said, "No, don't worry. You don't have to go. Maya is in no position to hurt anyone."

William looked at her as if trying to convince her that everything that he said was true.

"She cannot come to you," he continued.

"But we made a deal," said Rachel.

"I mean, I guess, technically, my parents made the deal. I just want to keep that word," continued Rachel.

They were silent for a minute before Rachel spoke again. "I need a new start anyway. I need to run away from my bad dreams, from the thoughts of what happened to all my beloved in this city. I just need to go."

"Go where?" asked William.

"I don't know. I've never been out of this city. Just plan to drive far away and go wherever it reaches, and try to find a job and a place to stay," said Rachel.

William moved a little closer towards Rachel. Rachel could feel his breath on her face.

"You won't be sacred out there alone?" asked William.

Rachel felt a little conscious of William standing so close to her.

"It couldn't be much scarier than here," said Rachel avoiding looking at William.

William continued to stare at her. "I came to say good bye. I'm leaving too," he said.

"Where are you going?" asked Rachel in a confused voice.

"I don't know. Anywhere is the same to me. Sleep in the day, live at nights. Makes no difference where I live," said William.

They were silent for a few seconds. Rachel looked at her bag and then at William. They both looked at each other, waiting for the other to speak.

"Shall I come with you?" asked Rachel.

William looked back at her confused.

"I will just stay in the town where you live. At least I know you will be there for me if I'm in trouble. I have nobody else to ask for help," said Rachel.

They were again silent for a few seconds. William looked at her surprised. He could see Rachel's eyes pleading to him.

"If you can't, it's fine. Just forget I asked," backtracked Rachel moving away from him.

He looked at her luggage and smiled back.

"If you're okay with the company of a vampire, I would love your company," said William.

He smiled after he saw Rachel smiling. It was clear that Rachel was happy to hear what William said.

"Thank you. Thank you so much," said Rachel. She jumped like a little child who was happy to get something new.

Chapter LIII

A New Beginning

Later that evening, Rachel and William decided to drive out of the city.

William took out the car, and Rachel placed the luggage in the trunk.

Rachel opened the door of the passenger side and sat in the car. She was very excited. It was the first time that she left the city.

William looked happy and content in her company.

The car reached the entrance of the city. They reached the board, 'Welcome to The City of Bridgeport'. Maya's crow was perched on it. William stopped the car near the board.

Rachel looked at the board and waved her hands at the board.

William started the car and they drove off into the night.

The crow followed them.

Chapter LIV

The Law of Karma

Back in the abandoned house, Maya lay in the casket. She opened her eyes, face red with anger. She tried shaking the casket, but every movement caused pain to her hands, every attempt to chant caused pain to her mouth.

Maya lay in the casket, with her eyes open, desperately thinking of a way to escape.